black girl love

by

anondra "kat" williams

First printing 2011

ISBN-13:978-1460971277

Published by LMInc
www.lmwrites.com
www.lesbianmemoirs.com

Printed in the U.S.A

to those that love me now & a few who loved me in the past

you feed me, thank you…

yellow girl…you give me wings

table of contents

black girl love

while singing softly
love
don't live here anymore
she wraps her legs
round my soul
cushioning me
from the world
as we do
black
girl
love
not sex
love
singing
moaning
listening
speaking
learning each other
accepting that
black
girl
love
hurts sometimes
pain filled pleasure
moments of living
telling tales
of now then and morrow
as she splits me
in half
in the middle of
only to seam me

in the middle of
the night
reminding me of
us
around tears of mine
as we do
black
girl
love

black girl love

purple

Purple. That was the color of the shirt she was

wearing when I first met her. I remember because I

thought it was loud and not cute, well at least not on her. It

was also just a little bit too small and the over abundance of

buttons and flaps made it appear to be some military reject

issue. I noticed her eyes as well, mainly because they

laughed when she laughed and I thought that was different,

well at least in my circle of friends, pretend and otherwise.

Thinking back on it months later the shirt suited her.

The boldness of the color matched her personality and the

flaps and pockets were just an indication of all the hidden

little pieces of her I would come to know. Love wasn't a

thought. She interested me, though more as a friend at first.

Not to say she was unattractive. How can mocha tinted skin

encasing a trim slim frame with a southern black girls' ass

be unattractive? It can't, so she wasn't.

After that first meeting I found myself running into her everywhere. I even jokingly accused her of stalking me. She laughed, her eyes did not. We exchanged the requisite phone numbers and emails eventually. Occasional texts and forwarded emails led to us calling before events to see if the other was putting in an appearance which lead to the heck why not save gas and go together conversations.

Speaking of conversations, we shared many of the late night variety. Politics, sex, books, sex. We always came back to sex, a lack of in my case and an over abundance in hers. I wasn't jealous, well not at first. I liked listening and giggling as she over shared. I don't think either of us noticed at first how she would run home from these "experiences" to tell me about them. We both noticed when I tired of hearing them.

Last week was the first time I said no when she wanted to go into detail about her latest. I pointed out in a sarcastic whisper, "If it was so great, why call me after?" She heard me. She pointed out that I didn't want to come out to play, at least not with her. Silence followed, five minutes or more before I finally said "I do," again in a whisper. She heard me.

Last night we played. We saved gas once again by driving together to dinner. Not a date per se because we were still friends. Nothing unusual happened at dinner, at least not on the surface. We talked, we ate and occasionally we touched. My hand resting on hers as I excitedly told her about a moment at work earlier in the week and a possible promotion. Our fingers touching as she passed the salt and again as I passed her the butter. Actions we've done casually many times before with no afterthought. This time every contact was followed with a pause in conversation, a slight lingering of touch.

After dessert was done and the bill was paid she asked me, "Why now?"

"Purple," was my response. The raising of her eyebrows indicated that might not be a good enough reason or that more was possibly needed, so I gave more.

"You wore purple the first time I met you."

That answer must have been good enough because the eyebrow went down, she stood up and we left, no longer just friends.

black girl love

buddies

We were friends at one time, soon after we became friends with benefits. Not the type you are thinking about but good ones none the less. We switched nights, if the other was busy. We both had keys. Come late, leave whenever. We were friends.

We were bed buddies.

Simple really, neither of us was involved and hadn't been for some time. We both missed the cuddling, the sharing of warmth along with the touch of another human during the night. A hand resting casually on hips covered in cotton, sometimes. Warm air blowing softly and evenly from thick lips, that were once thought to be too big, but are now just right. The joy of waking up in the morning to sunshine soaked sheets shared by another. Like I said it was the simple things we missed.

We devised a plan one late night over the phone, after
another night alone. I'm not attracted to her. She's not
attracted to me. The plan was simple, two nights a week, week
days only, we sleep together. Not sleep together, sleep
together but actual laying down covered in sheets with
a questionable thread count, alarm going off in the morning,
rushing to get to the 9 to 5 sleep. Genius if you ask me and I
was amazed we hadn't thought of it sooner. I shared our
 decision with friends who didn't quite share in my
enthusiasm. I explained to them we were friends and were not
attracted to each other. She's thicker than I normally go for
and I'm to femme for her.

It was a simple, easy and beautiful plan and till it became
complicated. I'm still not sure if it was the first night or the
second night when I realized her skin was as soft as brown
butter. At first it was just the patch of skin on her right side
below her tenth rib and above her pelvic bone. I found this out

when her baby t-shirt crept up. I didn't push it up. We were spooning. She sleeps better that way, me spooning her, she told me. I didn't mind.

I soon discovered there were similar brown butter soft patches all over, all over. I tried not to touch but my hands traveled and the front of my thighs melded to the back of hers, skin touching. We were spooning, she sleeps better that way. I didn't mind. She falls asleep quickly I learned, me not so much. I was distracted, adjusting.

I didn't realize till maybe the fourth night of being bed buddies that the shea butter she wears after showering lingers on me, around me all through the next day, lining my nostrils. Still there after I've scrubbed and soaked for hours. Traces of her, I had never noticed before. She laughed when I mentioned it and said that the scented oil I rub my body in, seeps into her pores and she was starting to like it. Shea butter, oil and us... we mix well.

On the tenth night when she neglected to tie her hair back

my dreams were infused with guava, mango and passion fruit.

I woke to her locs covering my face and painting images on

my sleepy canvas. She said later that I played in them while

sleeping, that I smiled while tugging on them slightly. That's

what woke her up, she says. I believed her. I didn't share my

dream of us being more than friends, hence the tugging

and smiling.

Friends asked if the bed buddy arrangement was working

out, a few even mentioned finding a bed buddy of their own. I

told them it was, at least on the surface. I didn't share that I

spent most of the week trying to recover lost sleep from the

nights she did stay over. I didn't share the mornings that

found us doing things we shouldn't have, things that weren't

part of the agreement.

She mumbles in her sleep and occasionally says my name.

She touches me in her sleep, in places that she shouldn't but

I've never stopped her. I keep finding patches of brown butter.

I licked my fingers last night after finding another butter

patch. I thought it would have a taste. It did; shea butter, oil

and her.

We are bed buddies.

The twelfth night I didn't sleep, neither did she.

black girl love

graduation

He's graduating today, my little nephew that is. Guess he's not so little anymore at well over six feet and 200lbs. Yeah like I said, he's not so little anymore. Graduations are special and for this one I traveled over 600 miles to be here, late. Sitting with strangers was not how I envisioned celebrating my nephew's graduation, surrounded by brown, yellow and a combination of both faces while searching the masses looking for the ones who resemble my own. My confusion or distress must have been obvious because she said something. She being the sista next to me. She being the one who has occupied the other part of my mind that isn't too upset to be sitting next to a buttercup fantasy.

She asked me if I was alright. I smiled before responding, "Yeah, just slightly stressed."

"Stressed about what?" was her obvious response.

"The flight here was late and that lead to issues with the car rental people which caused me to arrive here even later and now I can't sit with my family." I responded with a slight laugh at the end. Saying it out loud had slightly minimized the severity of the situation. I was here and that's what counted.

So I settled back in the not so comfortable stadium seating to watch my oldest and dearest nephew grace the stage. She settled back as well, shoulders touching slightly. Neither of us moved away. I smiled, she smiled.

"Sorry for being so rude, I dumped my problems on you before I introduced myself. I'm Elise and you are?"

"No need for sorry, I'm naturally nosey. I'm Shontay but my friends call me Shay."

"So what do near strangers call you?" I asked with a slightly, flirtatious tone. Hey, you don't win if you don't try was always my motto.

"Well they can call me anytime," she answered back

with a toothy grin. I couldn't help but laugh out loud. She got me one better.

"So Shontay, sometimes called Shay and called by strangers anytime, who are you here wishing the best for?"

"My goddaughter, she's the one with the rhinestones on the top of her cap."

We both laughed out loud at that.

"You know she's going to have to pay for that right?"

"No, I am," she belly laughed. "It's part of my graduation gift to her, the cap and hopefully not the gown. We stayed up for hours last Saturday night making sure they formed her initials perfectly."

"Oh so you are the good godmother?"

"I'm the best," this was said with a slight lifting of the shoulders and head. No false modesty here.

"Well best godmother you are in good company because I am the best aunty in the world."

Again we both laughed.

Silence settled in once again around us with a slight tenseness in the air, at least on my part. Quick checklist reminder to self, I am here to celebrate my nephew's graduation not to pick up the hot chick that I happen to be sitting beside.

"So what are you doing after the graduation?" Did I just say that? Did I not just remind myself of my purpose for being here?

"Well we're having a party for my goddaughter that probably won't last too long. What about you, what are you doing?"

"The same, I'm going to kick it with family till around 9 before meeting up with friends for a late dinner."

"Friends huh?" said in a slightly deeper questioning tone than what is normal for near strangers.

"Yeah friends, I don't live here anymore so whenever I hit town its dinner and dancing with a heavy dose of reminiscing. You are more than welcome to join me or rather us." The us was added quickly at the end because no one likes rejection.

"Dinner and dancing with strangers sounds like fun, count me in," this was accompanied by a surprising hand extension that I gladly accepted... firm, confident and dry with short, real nails. After the handshake, that possibly lingered longer than expected in polite society between near strangers, she reached in her purse and retrieved a business card which she politely handed me.

"Here's my number, call or text me and let me know when and where and I'll meet you there."

We parted ways soon after the graduation, with the agreement that I would do that when I left the family gathering to head to the other *family* gathering. I didn't tell her what was really going on but I figured just by agreeing, she would be comfortable either way. Though I have to admit I was hoping that she was family or at least a family friendly, the kind of family friendly that ended with her becoming family. The clothes she wore didn't really give me an idea nor did my gay meter go "beep beep."

I sent the agreed upon text a little before 9pm, "Hi Shay, it's Elise, we're meeting at I *"Jr's"* in 30 minutes hope to see you there."

I didn't look back at my phone til after I arrived at the local restaurant slash gay bar that everyone frequented, because I really didn't want to be disappointed if she couldn't come. That was a really long 20 minute drive and after greeting all my friends I finally got up enough courage to look at my phone.

"kk see you there."

That was enough to bring a huge smile to my face and questions from the group of friends at the table. I told them I had invited a friend that I met today at the graduation but before I could go into details I felt a hand come to rest on my right shoulder. It was her… a her that it turns out they knew. There were greetings all around as they exchanged hugs and kisses while I stared in slight shock. Turns out Shay was the friend that I was not interested in meeting the last time I was in town which was about six months ago. I was going thru a break up and the friends thought introducing me to someone new was the right medicine for a broken heart. I passed. One due to the rebound factor and the second was due to no desire to ever live in my hometown again. Why bother meeting someone who might make me change either of those thoughts?

After them laughing at my dumbstruck expression and the situation, the evening turned out to be fun, with dinner and drinks followed by dancing. Shay spent most of the evening letting me know she was interested with slight touches here and there. I wasn't surprised when she invited me back to her home for drinks and a "continue to getting to know you" conversation after the evening ended. I accepted.

Maybe moving back home might not be such a bad idea after all.

black girl love

stories

She came over last night, seeking conversation of an intellectual nature. Yeah I laughed to when she invited herself over by saying those exact words. The conversation moved along rather lazily as I flipped channels, in between stealing glances, in between pretending I was listening to her latest rant about something or other. I don't really know what because I was distracted. I was distracted by her and her smile, her laughter and her scent. Her body was a whole 'nother distraction.

In the midst of her talking, she started walking, almost strolling, around the living room touching my personal "stuff." Everything in my home is my personal stuff, I'm a Taurus. My attention focused on the physical movement of her and I wasn't sure if that was a good thing or not but she definitely had me.

Remote stilled. She picked up my elephant statue made of soap stone, rubbing her fingers over it slowly, then rapidly while comparing the feeling being produced, smoothing the smoothness. I could see it in her face, read it in her eyes that she liked it; liked the feeling of fingers on cold stone, turning warm. I could also tell she wanted to taste it like a child. I wanted to be that statue.

When she put it down I wanted to grab it and feel her warmth, lick it. I needed to know what soapstone and her tasted like together and apart. She kept moving in a circular pattern around the room, fingers touching, gliding over a vase here, a picture there, touching another statue and various knickknacks. They were all capturing her scent, warmth and flavor. I wanted to be them all. I wanted to be the picture whose corner she straightened. I wanted to be the glass ball she tossed none to carefully in the air. I just wanted her to touch me, haphazardly with good intentions.

She stopped at my bookshelf, the center one, my soul, the essence of me. She knows this as her fingers lightly traced the spines of my favorites. The ones I cherish, bent and broken with highlighted passages of life. I've read from a few to her. She strokes those knowingly, intimately. Still talking and sharing with the occasional small lapses into silence as she rubs my spirit.

She pulled one of my favorites from the shelf, "Love" by Toni Morrison. The opening sentence seems to always put me in a place, a space. She turned to the first page, fingers pointing out the path most taken

I read along with her silently.

"The women's legs are spread wide open…so I hum."

She laughs softly, no question on my part as to why, we both know why. She asks slyly for recommendations. I suggest what's in her hand and a few more. She's a reader like me and owns quite a few that are stored in my soul.

Finally she comes to sit back down, closer than before. I wonder if she can smell me and the excitement that's lying just beneath the surface of friend for the evening. She reaches over and grabs the remote from my hand but never quite releases my hand. She rubbed me or rather the center of my palm and the length of my index finger slowly, then rapidly. I could see it in her face while reading it in her eyes. She liked it, she liked the feeling. Wanted to taste it like an adult, I hoped.

The entire time we were still talking though about what, I know not. Almost felt like a Charlie Brown moment, I was hearing but not hearing. Looking back I'm wondering if she thought she was soothing me, calming me like you would a baby, a hurt child or your favorite pet. If so, the opposite effect was achieved. Her rubbing slowed, the channels stopped turning and her voice and her story paused or was it petered out? In the end she was silent. I waited for something, a sign, a movement from injured prey. She dropped my hand while sighing and said a quiet thank you.

I wasn't expecting that. A kiss maybe or a hand being placed where it shouldn't in mixed company, in a crowd or in front of your mama, but a thank you? That threw me for a loop so I swallowed and asked.

"What are you thanking me for?"

"For listening to me," she said with a slightly goofy grin in place.

"You're welcome." I responded slightly confused and not really sure what my next step should be. Should I be a gentlewoman and let the evening end on a high note or should I let the fat lady sing a much higher note, possibly in the prone position?

I leaned back slightly while observing her, waiting and watching. I think I watch too much of those nature channels or something because I felt animalistic and predatory. Inside I was wondering how can you stalk what is already on your table? Attack and devour what's already spread for my enjoyment and waiting for me to "dine" at leisure?

I could tell she was finally getting the hint that maybe just maybe things weren't as friendly as they appeared. She has this habit of licking her lips, actually not both and not in entirety just the right corner of her bottom lip when she's nervous or excited. The tip of her tongue pokes at it in a harassing manner. I'm jealous of her bottom lip. I want to be harassed while being prodded and licked. I've pointed this particular habit out to her before and like before I think she does it on purpose.

I watched and I waited for a signal and it came. Subtle and you really had to be there and you have to know her to see and understand. Her tongue paused and stilled for a heart beat more than was needed. She wanted me to look and she wanted me to want to know that she wanted me and that she knew

I wanted her.

So I pounced. Close to attacking but that wasn't the game we were playing that night. Felt like I was moving in slow motion but I know within seconds I was on her. I pushed her back flat on the couch. I knew what I wanted and I was going in for it. I wanted her tongue. That pink tease. Grabbed it with my teeth and felt a slight smile on her lips. Not for long. Sucked just the tip inside and got an instant reaction. Gasp from her and heat from me.

Hot slow heat, the kind that builds slowly, that had been building from the initial words exchanged. Touching my stuff was touching me, foreplay. The fire… the heat starts out, barely, almost not noticeable and then surprise, surprise the forest is burning around you. Metaphorical trees crashing with my weight on her pressing in, we are both accepting gravity.

Sucking on her lips and tongue while my hands explore... touching lightly, cotton, buttons and yes some heated skin… wanting to be rougher because that's my nature, wanting to be sweeter because that's my nature. She was reaching to, slightly distracted by her finger nails running furrows in my back through my shirt. How do you pull away while pushing in? I was doing it. I was grinding my hips and breasts while my bowing back was reaching for her fingers.

Wanted, no needed skin on skin so I pulled back slightly. Don't get me wrong it was hard. Her mouth was warm and we fit to together so perfectly, no gnashing of the teeth and bumping of the noses. She moved with me. Decision made, again. Conversation of a physical nature continued. Our bodies spoke in languages learned long ago, from birth of self, acceptance of self. We exchanged life stories thru skin scars and blemishes. Fingers singing songs of the R&B abandoned, not needed in the story telling process. Warmth invading still as friction increased, as need increased while release came slowly from tongues heavy with words and fingers switching to jazz melodies that we were co-writing, staccato tones.

She came over last night, seeking to share stories. We wrote one together instead.

black girl love

decisions

I felt it first, casually while making love one night, in the middle of licking on skin that I know almost better than my own. Scars, bruises and bumps, I know the story behind each one. I've listened as she shared and we bonded over everyone, been there when a few were created. This was a new one. I stopped, we stopped, pausing as life became sharper, the moments of. Her family has a history of this and really we should have expected this but that doesn't mean acceptance of.

Her reaction on the other hand was the opposite of what I did expect. She accepts with a shake of her head, hair falling to hide her face as she tells me that she isn't going to the doctor to find out if the lump means anything. What will be, will be.

That was two weeks ago, two weeks of the same

argument, loud tones, tears falling and fighting. More fussing really but who's splitting hairs?

"Why not?" I asked for what had to be the fifth time that day, the millionth in the last two weeks.

"I don't want to. I mean why bother? I'm going to die whether it turns out to be true or not, everyone dies and if it's not true then I'll be all right," she replied in the same steadfast matter of fact tone that seemed to have been in existence only in the last two weeks. At least that's what my mind said, all I know was the smiling voice that I loved was gone, replaced by this automation recording that kept repeating "no" to me if she responded at all.

"What about me? Us?" again the same question asked multiple times in one day. The answers she's given aren't right, at least not to me.

"What about you and us? You act like I'm leaving or dying tomorrow. It took my aunt months to die."

"What kind of shit is that to say?" I asked, not even

angrily, because I knew the why's and what's.

Though they didn't matter to me, what happened to them couldn't happen to her. I wouldn't allow it.

"It's the fucking truth! What do you expect me to say or do? Oh I know, that tomorrow I'm going to skip happily to the doctor so they can run tests and tell me something we already know." She jumped up from the lounging position in her favorite chair, the closest chair to the TV and farthest from the kitchen.

"You know what happens next? I'll tell you what happens next. First thing the 'doctors' are going to want to do is start cutting and taking stuff out all in the hopes of maybe. Maybe if we remove this, you'll get better. Oh wait, that didn't work, lets remove this. Cut here, cut there, till finally there's nothing left to cut. Well maybe I'm good now, good enough that I'm not doing that." All this was said and punctuated with her stalking through the family room in our home, each word getting louder with each step. Finally, a reaction I can understand, something expected, anger. The silent acceptance I couldn't accept or fight, this I could.

"I spent months watching them cut on my sister, cutting pieces of her soul every time she went into that hospital. She was never the same after that first operation and by the last one I didn't even recognize her anymore. I don't think she even knew who she was toward the end. She spent the last year of her life fighting something when she could have been doing something like loving her husband and kids, making memories." She finally stopped in front of me, grabbing me up, holding me close as she whispered the rest in my ear.
"I want to spend my time making memories with you, the kids and the rest of the family. What I don't want to do is to spend whatever time I have left going back and forth to the hospital for maybe's, could be's and this might fucking work."

Tears falling as I listen. She listens.

She's going tomorrow and then we decide on what memories to make of us, for her, for me and for the kids. We can fight and make memories together, if she lets me.

black girl love

lifetime

Morning surprises at my age are never nice and this was no exception. I am a creature of routine, have been since recognizing that routine makes me feel, well secure. I know that sounds odd but I have to do the same things in the same way to feel as if my life is in control. She knows this.

I wake, slowly but I'm not a snoozer. Internal alarm says rise and shine at 6am, no matter the day. I lay there and think on moving body parts that are slowing down and wearing out when they use to spring back from daily living as if welcoming the wear and tear.

Once I throw the covers off, I pride myself on not laying down again till bedtime that night. No naps for the elderly here. After rising, it's the daily a.m. washing of body, brushing of teeth and sometimes making of bed. I'm not a neat freak.

I like to eat a light breakfast, two eggs and two pieces of bacon or a bowl of oatmeal. I drink two cups of coffee, one while cooking and one while eating. As I said I'm a creature of habit. By 8:00am I'm usually sitting in my favorite chair facing the boob tube with laptop in hand or rather lap. I start by checking my email, sometimes I read the spam ones just because I'm bored and maybe penile pills really do work.

This morning I had a surprise when I opened up my email account. Down the list past all the penile implants, supposed job offers and women from Russia saying they want a new friend there was an email from an address that I hadn't seen in years. From a person I hadn't seen in at least a decade. I paused for more than ten minutes before finally clicking on the email itself and reading words I knew I really didn't want to.

Hey Stranger,

I know you are sitting there with your cup of coffee in hand, in front of the TV checking your email. I wanted to reach you this way vs phone because you might not answer and what I got to say shouldn't be left on a voice mail.

I know you are surprised to hear from me and I'm slightly surprised that I'm writing you but life is full of surprises, good and bad. I got a bad one a year ago. After waking up not feeling so great for a few months I finally decided to use that Medicare card and go to the doctor. He was recommended by Roberta, you remember her? Well I go in there expecting a pill or two to add to my collection of high blood pressure and diabetes medicine. Turns out it's something a little more serious than popping a pill for this illness. I'm dying Rae. They trying to tell me that I can battle this cancer but I'm tired of them cutting and I'm tired of them feeding me more bullshit than a little bit about this treatment and that new treatment but mainly I'm just tired. So I decided to stop the extra stuff, you know the chemo, surgery and pills.

Like I said I'm dying. They are "giving" me a few weeks but then again they said that a few months ago. Who knows, either way I'm giving myself a little longer just to surprise them all.

So I'm writing this long ass email to say my goodbyes. Only writing a few to those who I loved, once. To those who loved me, once. If you never knew it, now you know. I loved you more than I loved myself at times, which is where the problem started. I figured out too late that you can't love someone else without loving yourself first. Never works. I wish I had seen the light then, so I could explain to you better the whys of why I just couldn't get it together. Why I couldn't come out

*just then. Why... hell you know the other shit. No need to drag
this out, like I said they only giving me a few weeks.*

*I don't expect you to come here like some knight in dull armor
or anything like that but I do ask that you keep an eye on my
kids for me. They well grown but I still worry that they gonna
be alright once I'm gone. Michael thinks he's found himself
finally and that girl of mine thinks fucking everything that
moves is the way to go. She looking for a "baller" at forty. I
told her ballers want 20yr olds but she ain't listening. You
know they still ask about you every now and then.*

*Like I said, I don't want to drag this out. Just check on my
kids every now and then.*

I love you, always have, always will,

Shirley

After wiping the still running tears from my face I

pushed the laptop to the side. It's time to pack up some things

and head out. A few weeks or a few months who knows,

guess we'll find out together.

black girl love

love

She said she loved me today while walking from the house to the car, slid it in while kicking a rock out of her pathway and avoiding a frog that happened to cross at the same time. I heard her over the sounds of cars passing by, kids squealing, birds chirping and my heart beat suddenly increasing. I answered with a slightly mumbled affirmative echo ending in "too."

We are an interesting couple and have been for a year without that word being mentioned. Initially focused on similar goals, likes and dislikes, tired of doing what had been done in the past. We approached this relationship different than the others.

Analyzed from all angles while debating on the likely hood of success we decided after all the number crunching that we would work out. Household chores decided upon, life expectations listed, sex organized and committed to.

We were doing it, living it and today she says she loves me.

Now what? Emotions involved, possibly always there but not acknowledged. We were trying something new dammit and now she done fucked that up.

She loves me.

I love her.

Fuck.

Now what?

black girl love

hungry

She wants me to mentally
fuck her pain
away

pretend we more than
just a two night stand
memories of

and im not a wound licker
dried blood clot tender
so I pass this time
while explaining why
as she puts me
once again
on the sidelines
of her life
catching drip drops
of her

she's starting to bore me
and the hunger in me
isn't being fed
mental rumbles
echoing in a space
long ago occupied by her

so why even bother
sitting on
sidelines
frontlines
by her side

it isn't something that
interests me
anymore

did I mention I'm bored

or should I stress
we've been here before
easing pain with
band aids of fake love
fake want
fake wetness seeping
from pens
of invisible ink

she says I understand her
like no other
and I say
she misunderstands me
like no other

pretending once again
we friends
till silence finds us again
time passes again
and we part once again

im hungry
she feeds me no more

black girl love

breaking

She called and I answered for the last time. She was asking questions while expecting no real answers, though I answered, as best I could. I answered mainly in mono-syllables till she tired of asking and started demanding responses as to the why. A "why" that really can't be answered with a simple "because" and a "I just don't know," at least not in her eyes. Was I possibly pushing the situation by not giving her the answer she sought, the one she needed to hear? Truth or not. Her reaction said definitely not. The clicking of the phone is still slightly ringing in my ear. I should have expected this reaction. It's not like I don't know her and how she reacts to any situation not being lead by her, defined by her. She overreacts, kicks and screams when a simple yes or no would suffice.

Here she comes now racing down the highway in route for a face to face conversation, confrontation. Looking for answers she's going to get this time, make me give, is really more like it. I'll let her for the last time. I owe her that, maybe. We both led us here, recognizing truth while admitting wrong. I've done that and it's time. It's time to end this shit. We've been here before and we've moved past this before. This time things are different, I'm different and she, she hasn't changed.

The sound of a car door slamming outside tells me everything I need to know. I know this is going to end with fussing, cussing and my shit breaking. Like I said, we've been here before. I run to open the door to prevent early visible breakage from the outside, because I know her and knocking isn't really on her list of things to do tonight. Well, knocking me around maybe. I open and dash back to open ground in the living room, seeking plenty of room to hopefully prevent being cornered. I guess the open door must have slowed her down, killed her expectations because she walked in slowly, with measured steps, eyeing me and the room, looking for me and her. She wasn't there. Stopping halfway in still looking around she asked.

"Where is she?"

"I told you on the phone she wasn't here." I was trying hard not to answer with an attitude but she was pushing it just by being in my house like she owned it and I was the visitor.

"Why isn't she here? I mean you fucking her and all, why not be here on a Saturday night with MY girlfriend?" I just blinked, thinking the question was more rhetorical than anything.

"So what you can't answer me now?" This was said with forward motion physical and vocally, enough for me to back up a step or two and hurriedly say something to hopefully mute this situation.

"She's not here because I didn't invite her here."

"Oh so you invited her in the other times you were fucking her? The other times you started arguments with me

to keep me away from here and to keep you away from me?"
Forward motion still, I see her body almost setting itself up to
spring, spring at me.

"What do you want me to say? Yes, I invited her.
Yes, I fucked her. You know this already so why are you
here?" I answered thinking maybe the real truth will make her
happy, get her to leave.

"I'm here to stare the bitch in the face who cheated on
me, that's why I'm here!"

I think the bitch comment did it, later on, looking
back while speculating with friends as to what really set
things off it had to be that word.

"Oh so I'm a bitch now? Well I'm the same bitch that
carried your ass for six months when you didn't have a job.
I'm the same bitch that's been dealing with you trying to
figure out if you're a lesbian or some other shit for the last
year. Transgender my fucking ass! I'm also the same bitch
that knows your sorry ass cheated on me with my so called

best friend. So yeah I'll be that bitch. What should we call you? Oh I know he-bitch."

Maybe that was the word? Who knows, actions followed soon after, I do know that. Grabbing and tugging leading to a quick illegal exchange between two who once professed undying love and swore never to do this to each other. Parting gifts of the permanent kind as hands were being laid on, not in prayer, till we stopped. Stopped fighting that is followed by tears being shed while fucking for the last time.

She was begging on the down stroke and seeking redemption on the upstroke. Attempting insertion of her into me beyond fingers and tongue, it's worked before. Not anymore though the trying is good, that never was our problem. The question of why was being answered even as we cum. I don't love you anymore because I don't and she, yes she, is a reason but then again so am I. You are the main reason. I'm the main reason.

Afterwards we pulled apart…sticky with answers mixed with cum and more questions that wouldn't be answered at least by me. I was done. We were done, done breaking up for the last time.

black girl love

bruises

She promised after the last time, that that would be the last time. It wasn't. I knew it wouldn't be because it wasn't the first time she had made that promise. It wasn't the first time I had agreed over tears and healing bruises to understand, accept, and forgive. Forgive that her love for me is so intense that it leads to slung hands around bruised from the past necks, shoulders, and arms.

She promised the time before the last time to seek counseling. She promised that we would seek counseling a treatment of some sort. I made an appointment, she didn't show. It wasn't her fault, life and living it kept us both busy and that day just happened to be really busy. I should have planned better. Should have planned for a day with no work for either of us, no bills to be paid, no dinner to be cooked. No living.

She promised once to apologize to my mother for abusing her daughter. She wrote it down, word for word what she was going to say. I said mail it. "No," she said, "This has to spoken face to face." I didn't ask for that. I didn't expect it and wasn't surprised when it didn't happen, the letter or the apology.

She promised me the moon, sun and the stars and delivered me to the hospital ER more than once. I accepted it as my worth. I needed to learn how to love her better, accept her more. I tried. I tried to anticipate what would make her happy, sad and most of all mad. Mad enough to turn from words to actions.

I remember the first time we fought. It was a simple push really after I said something that she didn't like. We were both surprised by her reaction. She apologized and I let it go as a one off thing that wouldn't happen again, till it did. The second time was a push again, followed by a slap. Again we were both surprised, me more than her. She apologized again but added that it was my fault this time and told me to watch my mouth. I slightly agreed, I mean maybe if I did shut up more than her hitting me wouldn't have happened. I believed that till the fourth or fifth time when she hit me after she had a bad day and I was standing in the way when she walked in the door. I was standing there to give her a hug, instead I got a shove and a punch to the stomach. I don't greet her at the door anymore.

I don't do much of anything anymore. We fought once after I hung out with some friends. I got home later than she said I could. I was only thirty minutes over due and I called her and told her I would be late. She greeted me at the door by grabbing my neck and dragging me thru the house by my hair. She accused me of cheating and made me strip naked to smell me, smell her on me she said. Then she took what I didn't want to give anymore. That part wasn't new anymore either. She usually wanted sex after enforcing her point. I cut my hair.

She told me that my mother was trying to separate us when she questioned me about the bruises and weight loss. I told her that my mother loved me and loved her and didn't want us apart. She disagreed and backed it up with a beating every time I went to visit my mother. I don't visit her anymore. We talk via phone while I'm at work. She doesn't like me to be on the phone or computer when we are at home together. She took my cell phone one night after I got a text from a friend asking why I wasn't being "friendly" anymore. Said she was in our business too much. I didn't bother disagreeing it was easier to just accept.

It took me awhile, a few more bruises and broken bones, before accepting that I can't do this anymore. Love her that is and I told her. She didn't believe me and told me to sit my ass down before I made her mad. I expected that reaction. I had even prepared a response to that statement but before I could open my mouth, she hit me in it. I guess making her mad was becoming easier and easier. I took the hit and the many that followed, the sex after. It made it easier, easier to shoot her point blank and in the head. TV and the movie lies, the splatter wasn't that intense. The look she gave me though, that was intense. She actually looked scared and surprised. I imagine that's what I looked like many times. Eyes and mouth stretched wide and open ready to say anything, agree to anything to stop what's about to happen from happening. It never worked for me and didn't work for her.

I told her that I no longer loved her and that I was tired, tired of loving her. Told her this was the only way to end it because I knew she wouldn't just let me leave. I started to ask her what was it about me that made her not love me enough but I stopped. It was too late, too late for her and too late for us.

In life you have freeze frame moments. She really shouldn't have fallen asleep afterwards. She should have let me speak before, before that first blow, before the very first and the last one.   She didn't.

As I was pulling the gun from up under the bed, I thought on how heavy my arm was with the weight of it. How cold it felt in my grasp. I didn't think on not doing it and congratulated myself for putting the bullets in earlier before she made it home. It's the simple things.

I woke her gently, kissed her on her the back of her head before pushing on her shoulder. She turned over fussing and cussing, swinging would have been next but the gun stopped her. Freeze frame. Things could have been so different, should have been so different for us.

I pulled the trigger. She died. I had two bullets in the gun, one for her and one for me. I didn't use mine. There wasn't really a need anymore. That I didn't expect, all the planning I pictured them finding both of us spread out here. Instead they will just find her. I think I'm going to disappear for awhile, live life for the first time in a long time. I know they will eventually catch me and punish me I guess but it's no worse than anything she did to me. I can accept that. Momma will understand, daddy beat her till she couldn't take it anymore. I guess blood tells.

black girl love

addiction

I can still taste you
in the back of my throat

tried to erase it

finger pushed in
til I gagged
still not reached

drinking from your well
is something I can
no longer do

still thirsty from the last time
and the many times before that
as we both tried
me harder
I think

to grow my love
to seed yours

ground has grown dry
barren
no longer furtile
as we pretend

pretending that life is right
and we doing right by

being… here

time passes as
the need passes
for you
for us
cravings no longer
reached for in your arms

im passing on that hit
this time

black girl love

trying

January 07, 20..

Dear Diary,

I saw her today. She didn't see me as usual. I sometimes wonder if she has ever seen me, really seen me for who I am. She still has that walk. Head and shoulders thrown back while leaning forward, marching into greatness is what I called it. She was also smiling, but not at me. She looked happy unlike the last time I saw her. I hope she's forgiven me for that. I was going through some things and I know I shouldn't have taken my problems out on her. I wonder how her family is doing. They haven't spoken to me since then either. I miss them all and the big Sunday gatherings. Maybe I should send her an email just to say hi and let her know that I saw her today. I wonder if her email, home address or phone number has changed.

January 12, 20..

She wrote me back!!! I can't believe she took the time to write me back AND she even said I should have stopped her to say hi or waved or something. Next time I will. I'll stop her and speak. I should go back there tomorrow to see if she comes back by. No, no that would look weird. Besides she hasn't passed back that way the last three days. I wrote her back, telling her how I've been doing and my job and school. I also told her I wasn't dating anyone. I just wrote and wrote till I couldn't write anymore. I hit send before rereading or editing.

I'm trying, the new medication works wonders and I'm taking it like I'm required to every day; morning, noon and night. I keep telling the doctor that it makes me feel nauseous and that I'm so drained and tired from sleeping so much but he insists.

January 17, 20..

She hasn't responded to my last email. I know I shouldn't worry or be mad it's only been five days. She does have a life right? Maybe she's dating someone new. She was smiling at the lady walking with her. No, no she's only a friend. She would tell me if she was dating someone new. I told her I wasn't dating anyone. She can't be dating anyone. Maybe she's sick. That's probably what it is, she's sick. I wonder if she needs anything or if anyone is taking care of her. I wish she would have called when she got the first sign of sniffles. I live to take care of my woman!

At least I'm not feeling sick anymore. I took the last pill on Monday. I accidentally flushed the rest down the toilet. The doctor doesn't know everything. He doesn't know me plus I need strength so I can take care of my woman now that she's sick. I'm going to take some get well goodies over to her house, you know some soup, crackers and juice, a few books, magazines or even a movie or two.   Maybe I should call first. No, I think surprising her would be best. She's going to be so happy. I love her and she loves me.

January 18, 20..

No call today and no response to my email or the package. I'm really getting worried. I've called all the local hospitals and even the police department. They said that only the next of kin can file a missing person report. I've told them that she's my lover. They told me to stop calling or else. I've called her mom. She keeps hanging up on me and I'm not sure what her problem is. Doesn't she understand that I'm worried about her daughter? That I'm worried about my lover? Okay so technically she's not my lover anymore but we still love each other. You can't stop love and no one can stop my love for her. I know I messed up and I apologized.

She forgave me. She told me to speak the next time I saw her. She emailed me back once. I know we can move forward all she has to do is call me. Call me and let me know she's all right, that we're all right. I'm just trying to love her.

January 20, 20..

I can't believe she still hasn't called me! I go out of my way to buy her soup and juice and even take it to her home. She wasn't there but I left it outside with a note attached, letting her know it was ME thinking of her. Letting her know that I still love her. You would think she would at least call to say thank you. I've called her several times today and last night of course. Not once has she called back. I drove by her house last night. I even got out and rang the doorbell. I thought she was in there but no one answered. I stood outside in the cold rain for almost 30mins waiting on her, for her. Where was she? Probably out with that bitch she was smiling at.

I don't know why she wants to play these games. She knows I love her and that I'm sorry. I'm not that person anymore. I've changed. The doctors even said I've changed. They let me come home because I didn't fit in with those people at Chattahoochee. They were crazy. I wasn't. I'm not. I was just stressed out and needed a break. The job and her and life, the pressure of it all was getting to me. I even got my old job back. Trial basis but I know I'll make it, this time. I just want to make sure she is all right. All she has to do is call.

January 24, 20..

I love her! I love her! I LOVE HER! She called me today finally. She said she had gotten my care package and all the emails and voice mails that I left. She also said she's been out of town and busy with work and that she wasn't sick. It's a good thing that she wasn't sick. Still it was rude of her not to respond to any of my calls or answer her door last night. I know she was at home. I sat outside her house all night watching as she moved from room to room. I even went to her bedroom window and watched over her while she slept. It was opened slightly. She always did like a slight breeze while she slept.

Funny thing is she asked me if I was taking my medication. She probably guessed I wasn't because I've been so full of energy lately! I've sent her hundreds of cards via email and mail and some I even took to her home and slid under the door the last few nights. I placed a beautiful handmade one on her pillow today, after she left for work. I even left flowers on her car yesterday, they were from her backyard so I figured she would like them best. I made her a photo album filled with copies of all the pictures from back when we were happy, before I let my problems mess us up. I included some new ones of her leaving her home, going into work, leaving the gym, eating out with friends.

I would have done more but I'm broke. They fired me when I started missing days. I was worried about her when she was sick. She made me lose my job, but I know she will take care of me and we'll be together forever. I'll take care of the house, cooking and cleaning while she works. A perfect family with kids and a dog, she's allergic to cats. She thanked me for everything and then she asked me not to email her anymore or call her anymore or come by anymore. She told me she was trying to move on with her life. I told her that I'm just trying to love her.

January 25, 20..

I love her. I don't understand why she can't understand that. Why she couldn't see that I will love her forever. I tried to get her to understand that tonight when I went over there. I knew she didn't mean what she said yesterday. I know her mom or that bitch she was smiling at told her to say that. I could hear them in the background telling her not to love me anymore. I know that's what took her so long to email me or call me back, them stopping her and taking away her phone and computers. It's them not her, they are holding back our love. They are jealous spiteful human beings who don't understand real love, our love.

I tried to get her to listen to me. She kept asking me how I got in and then she started telling me I should leave. That now wasn't a good time for a visit. I told her I couldn't leave her again. I tried to explain. She wouldn't listen. She just wouldn't listen. I only held her down so she would shut up and listen. She was screaming and crying so loudly that I had to hit her to calm her down. You know like they do in the movies, only this time it didn't work. She didn't shut up and calm down she got louder. She kept screaming at me to let her go and to leave.

Why did she want me to leave? I was only trying to love her. I kept hitting her hoping that she would just be quiet for one minute. Enough time to let me talk. Enough time to

show her how much I love her. I kept on hitting her even

after she stopped screaming. I kept on hitting her even when

she started making these weird noises. Almost like a cat

being hit with a baseball bat. I miss Fluffy, she was allergic

to her so she had to go. Poor Fluffy, she made me do that to

her. She always makes me mad. She didn't return my phone

calls or respond to my emails for days. Making me worry,

stressing me out again. All the cards I sent and made just for

her! The roses that I handpicked…I can still see the scars

from the thorns and the blood that is still pouring down my

hands. All the photos I took of her laughing and smiling with

others. Never with me! Never with me! Now she wants to

cry and tell ME to leave! I can't. She knows that. I will love

her forever. She's mine forever. I kept on hitting her even

after I heard nothing from her, no pleas for me to stop, no

more asking me to leave. I kept on hitting her when it didn't

even feel like I was hitting her, a person… squishy, warm red stuff covering my hands. I hit her till I couldn't raise my hand anymore. I was tired. I laid down to rest. She was already asleep. Laying beside me like it should always be. I wrapped my arms around her waiting. Waiting on her to wake up so we can be together again.

I know now that she understands that I'm just trying to love her.

black girl love

you

all i ever think bout
is you
and sometimes
that's not a good thing
in the middle of
pain filled silences
as
visual representations of
me and you
flooding
eyes closed to the
truth of
me and you
no more
though I see
you trying
and I hear what
you saying
echoing
in between reality of
words already spoken
louder
so I move left
and you move right
we not dancing
just
stepping over

shit piles of
trust
love
hurt
pain
relationship
well past its expiration date
curdling
in this fridge
we built
not purchased
winter approaching
inside
and
out
wrapping self in blankets
of you
in the end
all I ever think about is
you

black girl love

two

Fire red, that's what I thought when I saw her. Fire red that was too hot to do anything except burn, burn everything good and bad around her. She didn't even try to pretend otherwise as she moved from group to group leaving little fires, destruction and chaos crumbs trailing.

I watched as she slowly made her way to my corner of the room, or rather my corner of the club. Watched as she flirted, tempted those she passed. Some worthy of a touch, a smile others not so lucky as they got an eye roll or a you're not worthy look from hard brown eyes.

Recognition came quickly once she was near enough to see past the strobe and neon lights peppering the club. I stood or rather moved off the wall I had been propped up on watching the show that was her and every other needy soul on a Saturday night in club Masquerade. We met halfway between nowhere. Slight smiles or grimaces depending on which angle you were looking from or if you knew the history behind us.

"Hi lady," I said.

"Hey stranger," she responded.

Both rushed greetings covering the other, slightly smothered by the music that was pounding from the speakers. She smiled more before saying, "It's been a long time. I didn't know you were back in town."

And it had been a long time, two years to be exact.

"Yea," I responded, "It has been a long time. I've been back about a month or two. Slightly surprised I hadn't run into you before now." I didn't tell her I had been looking over my shoulder for the last two months, looking into every car as it passed, staring at every woman with locs swinging hoping it was her.

"Well the number hasn't changed, nor has the address so if you really wanted to see me you could have." This was said as the smile faded along with the pretense and concern for those watching this live version of the L Word.

I could see the pain, still there bubbling below the surface looking to spill forth. It was a long time coming and this time I couldn't run, not like the last time. I thought of throwing a joke in the silence along the lines of I don't like talking to dial tones or ducking bricks but I had a feeling I would wind up covered in that drink she was holding. The drink was something new, she didn't drink two years ago. Said more than once that drinking was a weak woman's toy and she didn't need liquor or anything else to have a good time. So I stood there for a moment before agreeing with a slight head nod.

We continued to stand there both contemplating what next to be said. I was leaning toward just walking away and was two seconds from saying good bye, nice to see you, don't be a stranger when she asked the question I was dreading.

"Why?"

Shit now what? I can't run, I can't hide and every eye in the place felt like it was on us. I was stuck like chuck, a fucked up chuck. So I did what I should have done two years ago. I was finally honest and said everything I should have said then, got everything out in a rush, thinking if I didn't say it now then it would never come out.

"I wasn't ready. Being gay was so damn easy for you. You wore your rainbow gear like a badge of courage and shot the finger to everyone who didn't agree. I wasn't there yet and didn't know if I ever would be. It felt as if you were forcing me to be you, to be lesbian, to be a dyke whatever you want to call it." Deep breaths as it all came out.

"You were convinced my momma, my family would accept it, accept us. How would you know? You barely met my momma. So I bounced."

She stood there, in shock I think. Quiet. I could see her mind spinning absorbing what I had rushed to say. So I kept on talking, like a gusher.

"I kept telling you that I needed time. That you were the first woman and that love doesn't cure everything. But you wouldn't listen, just kept fucking pushing me into this idea of what "gay" was to you. I didn't want to hang with all your "gay" friends. I didn't want to come out at work and you dropping by and demanding a kiss before leaving sure wasn't going to keep it that way. I didn't want to go to Pride, shit I was still trying to figure out what a damn Pride was. You just wouldn't stop."

I couldn't stop talking though I could tell the shock had worn off and another emotion, anger was slowly coming to the forefront.

"So I did. I stopped us. I figured you would be alright. Figured the gay coalition or something would help you get over me, a non-gay. I wasn't your first and your ex's were always around the corner ready to jump back into something with you anyway." That last part was said with a sneer and a grimace. Those chicks were always a phone call or door knock away it seemed. Popping up at every moment they could. She said they were just friends. Who in the hell is friends with all their ex's? Said it was a gay thing. Some gay bullshit if you ask me.

At that I paused, took a look at her face again and took two steps back before recognizing that that might not have been the best move. Hunter and prey came to mind.

She moved two steps forward and a few steps more till we were almost within kissing distance, though that's not what I think she was trying to do. Matter of fact I'm positive that was the last thing on her mind. This was backed up by her hissed comments.

"Instead of just flat out saying I'm not ready to be with you or I don't think I'm a lesbian, you just ran? Instead of just saying you're rushing me or I'm not ready, you just up and disappeared from the damn city?" This was punctuated by her finger, nail and all emphasizing each question with a slight shove in the center of my chest.

"You told me you didn't like my friends because they were messy not because they were gay! You told me that your boss didn't like wives or husbands coming to the job, that it disrupted the work day or some shit like that so I believed you. I only asked to kiss you goodbye one fucking time! I asked you to go to Pride so we could hold hands in public and you could see and experience more couples likes us. Hopefully, see them making it, working things out."

She paused slightly but only to gather more air in her lungs, not to stop.

"Instead of saying anything your weak ass just bounces with no word, no letter, or email not even a fucking text message!"

She was getting louder and louder with each word and I was backing up more and more till I was pressed up against the wall I had been leaning on a few minutes earlier.

Yea we were the center of attention for sure now. Everything I tried to avoid by leaving two years ago was now happening in spades. I tried to get her attention along with calming her down by grabbing her arm. That was the wrong move, the fire that was her combusted.

She jerked her arm away with a flourish and while almost hitting me in the face in the middle of shouting even louder if that was possible. "You didn't tell me shit! All you wanted was your pussy ate and to leave the house before anyone saw you in the morning. That's what I got from you and still I tried. I tried to get you to see that it would be all right and that our love would weather the storm."

"Hell do you think you're the first person to realize they love women and come out of the closet?" This was said with a roll of heated eyes. I swear there were glints of red in there.

"My ex's were there telling me you weren't about shit but I told them no, she's just scared. So damn scared that you ran in the middle of night like the punk ass they said you were!"

By this time tears were falling and it seemed like the music had stopped and everyone was silent, staring at us and she continued to release everything inside.

"I begged your mother for your number, rode by her house, your apartment and job till I thought they would call the cops on me. Called your phone and sent emails and texts till I couldn't find the words to beg anymore and I got nothing from you. Now here you stand, like nothing ever happened. Like your bitch ass didn't just up and leave without a word, a call or a text."

Finally she took a step back and I foolishly thought this was all over.

"Yeah I'm wearing my rainbow badge and here's a fucking finger to you!"

That drink, that was new, mixed well with my shirt and jeans, starting to drip even before she walked away, heels clacking over music that ten minutes ago was loud as hell,

now on semi-mute bass only blasting or was that my

heartbeat?

I've seen her, see her now more clearly as she walks

away. I didn't before.

black girl love

sex

I miss good sex. You know the kind you think on all day, the kind that leaves your panties wet and your mouth dry. The kind that has you lost and confused at work, dazed as you manage to stumble thru the hours till you can get to her.

I miss that.

She, on the other hand, must not because I'm the only one complaining. Daily gripping, bitching and moaning that's me. Not proud but being honest. I need sex, good sex on a regular basis. Touching self gets boring and repetitive after awhile. I am an expert on that, nine months and counting since the last time pleasure was given by another. Sex is sort of symbolic of our relationship issues, being that is more visual than the others but still there.

No sex for nine months, no intimacy for more than that. I can't recall the last time I love you flowed from her lips to my heart or vice versa. We just do. Wake, quick air kiss good bye, work, home and pretend conversations over flickering screens and clacking keyboards before we lay it down for rest. A rest where we don't touch, pillows thrown in between to ease newly discovered back issues. Cement.

So here we are or rather here I am imagining good sex with another. Yes another. I am contemplating climaxing with another's lips on my lips and thinking that's not a bad thing. It's taken me months to get here, in this space, this place even. Here I sit waiting on her to arrive.

Here is a neighborhood bar/restaurant. Her is the she I met online. Yes online, it's like the new black or in this case the new gay. It started out simple enough with a compliment on a picture that I was fully clothed in. Before moving quickly or slowly depending on who you are asking, to emails private and work, texting because she just had to tell me something one day and an email just wouldn't do and finally talking. Talking after the air kiss as I traveled to work, lunch breaks spent soaking up words sprinkled lightly from a slightly deep voice and drive home fillers to carry me thru the night. Online instant messages til two am, text messages of I miss you at four am. We slowly fell.

I fought it till, well I stopped fighting.

Our most recent conversation led me to here, finally she would say. Today we were doing the usual drive home filler to get me through the night when she casually mentioned a new friend. She scared me with those words, so much so that I actually pulled off to the side of the road.

"A new friend?" I asked nervously.

"Yes."

"When did you meet her and why am I just now hearing about it?"

"She dropped me a line a few weeks ago on Faceblog, said she had seen me before out and about." Almost in a rush she got out the rest, "We started talking a little bit more recently and she wants to hang out sometimes. Honestly I wouldn't have even responded but I'm tired of sitting alone at home each night. And like I said we just friends." This last part was said almost angrily.

"So when are you and the new friend hanging out?" I asked with dread creeping in.

"This weekend. We're going to check out that new sushi place that I mentioned to you. You know the one I asked you to go to."

That hurt. She knows and I know that I can't be seen out in public with her, but then again that was the point. She's tired of waiting on me to end this with her.

"So you're just now deciding to tell me?"

"I didn't have to tell you at all. It's not like you care what I do on the weekends as long as I'm there when you can catch five minutes away from her."

That hurt even more.

"How can you say that? You know I care and I spend more than five minutes with you on the weekend!"

"Five minutes on the damn phone! We've been doing this for almost six months and I just started getting calls from you on the weekend last month and again that's only when she's not around, which isn't fucking often. I'm tired of this."

Silence. She said it, couldn't be taken back. Now what? I sat there, staring at the cars passing, windshield wipers keeping time with my heart beat as it sped up to match the increasing rain. Time passed as I listened to her breathing.

"I'm sorry." Is what I said when I finally spoke. "You're right. You shouldn't be at home alone and you shouldn't spend your weekends by yourself. I'm sorry I've put you through this. I'm sorry that I'm too fucking scared to just let her go and do what we've been talking about, working on. I'm sorry that I can't love you enough to give you up. I'm sorry that this friend can give you what you need, what I want to give you." I was crying by the last sentence. We've been here before, me crying and her being tired. I had a feeling this was going to be the last time. Her next words confirmed that.

"I'm sorry to. I love me enough to let you go. I need more, Terrie." She stopped speaking almost like the air had been sucked from her with those words, deflated.

Silence again sheltered us as I tried to find words to make her take those back, to get her to understand what she meant to me. I started speaking several times but nothing came out, everything seemed to have been said before except this.

"I'll end it tonight."

"Ok."

Silence again as I waited for more than just "OK." It didn't come. I guess actions do speak louder than words, so I spoke again.

"I'll meet you at Harry's on 5th hopefully in an hour or two, depending on how this works out."

"Ok, I'll see you then. Don't disappoint me, Terrie."

This was said with the tone of one who was disappointed by me before. Truth hurts.

"I won't, I promise." I meant that.

black girl love

seven

Seven years of togetherness today. Seven years of struggles, promises made and today she decides it's over, that she's had enough. Today she decided to tell me what the last nine months of distance have really meant, the late nights up on the computer while I slept in the next room, the constant texting and whispered conversations that ended when I came into the room.

I knew and really didn't need a confirmation I thought. After seven years I know her like I know myself, if not slightly better. I know that when she first wakes up she doesn't like to talk till after she has sat still at the foot of the bed for five minutes. I know that she's allergic to shrimp but can't resist a certain dish out at our favorite local spot, so I carry Benadryl in my purse on the off chance that we go there. I know her better than myself, so I knew this wasn't going to be the typical conversation full of problems that I would have the solution to. That was my role, problem solver, keeper of the family. I thought she was my partner in this till recently.

She walked in the door with the remnants of tears running down her face. I went to hold her, console her and solve the problem. She stopped me with an out flung arm. Turns out I was the problem.

"We need to talk," she said as if the words were being forced out.

"What about, why are you crying?" I asked playing the concerned partner role, slightly sincere because Terrie doesn't cry often, at least not in front of me.

"I'm done!" was the heated response, anger bubbling and spewing, drying tears that had started to appear again out of nowhere.

"Done with what?" I asked with more concern. Problem solver.

"This! This half ass relationship, this pretending we still care when we both know we really don't. We're just existing and I'm tired of existing with you. I want more from life, hell I deserve more from life. So I'm done." The last was said almost as if she expected me to argue or fight. I didn't. Instead I stood there and agreed in silence. My silence or the blank look on my face must have angered her because she started talking again this time saying things I wasn't expecting.

"I'm in love."

"Ok."

"I met her months ago and we've been talking, falling in love. She's tired of being the other woman and wants us to be together."

"Ok."

"She deserves better, I deserve better and I'm ready to give her all of me."

"All right."

"Besides I figured you wouldn't even notice if I was here or not any longer. We're barely living, waking and sleeping because it's routine, not because we want to. I can't remember the last real kiss we shared or the last time we touched each other except in passing in the bathroom."

"Ok."

"I want to be excited again about someone, get to know someone. Hell hug someone…"

"I said OK dammit! You want out, fuck it fine. Get your shit and go, just please stop with the sing song shit about being in love with some other woman. You think you're special because you found someone else to love instead of working on us. What? You want a damn cookie or something for wanting 'more.' I gave you more but your selfish ass couldn't see that!" It felt good to release on her so I continued by saying all the pent up things I should have said years ago.

"So fuck you and the new chick. I wish her well in

dealing with your moody ways, the putting yourself first by switching jobs every six months because 'they' don't understand you. Would it have killed you to wash a damn dish once or twice in seven fucking years? Pay a fucking bill without me begging first? You ever think I was tired after working overtime trying to cover all of our bills as you found yourself and your calling. I got a calling for you, it's called being grown. Go and be happy, I know I will be." I finally stopped to breathe and realized there was really nothing more to say.

My response obviously startled her, the content and voice level. We both stared in silence waiting for the other to make a move, words or actions. She finally did by turning around and heading back out the door she just came in.

"I'll be back tomorrow while you are at work to get some things and we'll talk later about separating everything." This was thrown over her shoulder as she exited. The door closing almost before the last word was out.

I stood there for another minute or more contemplating my life and changes made in less than five minutes. Honestly I can't blame her and a part of me is happy that she ended it instead of me. We've been running on empty for a long time, doing what we do, the usual surviving, paying bills and building a life that wasn't really living. We hadn't had sex in over nine months. My fault, her fault who knows, either way we weren't having it. It's funny how good sex can sometimes mask issues and cracks in a relationship. No sex points them out rather glaringly.

At least now I can meet my new friend for sushi this weekend with a clear conscience.

black girl love

seeking

Online dating is for the birds or rather in this case the chicken heads. I know that's not nice to say but the one's I've met have definitely fallen into the category of straight, pun intended, chicken heads. One chicken head actually asked me to pay her cell phone bill after exchanging one email. Hell I didn't even have her number. Another wanted to introduce me to her momma on the first date. It didn't help that she still lived with her momma, add to that the no job thingy and I could see where this was going. I don't think her momma had a job either.

When I met Terrie I thought I had finally met the right one; a beautiful, black, professional and employed female. The conversation we shared was great and we talked more bout books and films than about clothes and music. Not to say those are bad things to be interested in, just so happens they don't interest me much. Plus I have this thing for intelligent women and spelling well is a long forgotten talent it seems. Oh yeah I almost forgot, she was in a long term relationship and seeking "friends only." There was that minor element that I over looked from day one. She over looked it to.

We started out simply as friends online, liking each other's status messages, pics and videos. Gradually we moved to email exchange and that lead to cell phone number exchange. I'm not sure who sent the first text or who made the first call. I do remember the first time that I woke with her on my mind. The first night where the last voice I heard was hers as she whispered good night to me from her hiding place in the bathroom. I saved the first text where she said "I love you." It was after an all marathon session of texting and revealing one day while at work.

We didn't text much in the evenings, she had a girlfriend. A girlfriend who didn't treat her bad, she just didn't treat her right. I tried to treat her right or at least tried to doing what I could online, via text and phone. I gave her the attention she was missing at home. She gave me what she could and I accepted the scraps, bits and pieces of her at moments not always convenience.

Did I mention we've never met? Yep, I fell in love with some pictures and font, big font. Since she was just seeking friends and I had sort of given up on the dating game at the time it made sense that we never really met or tried to meet, at first anyway. We lived in the same city and knew some of the same folks but had never really been in the same space at the same time. After falling in love, we made a point to continue this. I wasn't sure if I could handle seeing her with her girlfriend and she wasn't sure she could handle seeing me at all.

I'm sure you see where I'm going with this. I didn't. I didn't see that nine months after exchanging likes and trading comments online that we would be here. Here being me seeking someone else finally and her deciding that she has found me, finally. I guess that should be more of she decided to leave her for me finally. I'm happy. I should be happy. Did I mention we've never met right? I sorta wished we had did that before she decided to leave ol girl. I mean what if it doesn't work out? What if we don't click in person? What if the online attraction turns into offline flatline?

We're supposed to meet tonight at Harry's after she tells the girlfriend it's over. I'm still not happy over how we got here. It wasn't like all of a sudden she decided she couldn't live without me, it was me admitting to having a date this weekend that pushed her over the edge. Leaves me wondering how long we would have continued down this pathway without any decisions being made. I'm thinking a long damn time.

I was honestly looking forward to the date this weekend. I met her online too. Yeah I know me and these online chickens. This one seems different. For one she wants to meet relatively quickly. We just started talking a few weeks ago and already she's like let's do something. We haven't really discussed much about what the other is looking for, just talked books and current events. I mentioned Terrie to her and she mentioned something about some girl. I didn't really ask much for detail besides I figured if she hit me up she must be single. She works a lot so I was sort of geeked that she requested a day off just to hang out with me. I guess I should text her and tell her I can't meet her after all. I don't know, maybe I should wait till after this meeting tonight at Harry's.

I'm feeling slightly overwhelmed right now and thinking I should have asked Terrie a few more questions about what meeting up tonight means. I mean are we a couple now? Is she moving in with me tonight? Hell no, I'm not

106

ready for that. Damn this isn't what I thought it was going to be. Shit! After nine months I should at least get some good sex out of this, right? Maybe it's not worth it.

black girl love

she calls it black girl love

She calls it black girl love
And I see bare ebony feet drudging through red clay
Dust coating her full lips
And sweat kissing her forehead...

She calls it black girl love
And I am taken back to my first time
Pain coupled with pleasure licking the line of uncertainty

She calls it black girl love
And I become consumed with the sway of her hips
The way her split smells after 8hrs of being bare
And trembling fingers fighting their way through gates they
are told not to go

She calls it black girl love
And I see myself in her arms
Nestled against her breast
Whirling my fingers through her locks
and masturbating to the rhythm of her breath

She calls it black girl love
And I instantly find myself exposed
Naked before her
Shedding my costume
Removing my mask
Slipping into my weakness
And embracing my ugliness

She calls it black girl love
And I relinquish my will to fight
Surrender my heart
Talk in my real voice
and pick up my pen

She calls it black girl love
Innocent
Sweet
Pure
Salty...

She calls it black girl love
And I just call it love...

by spoken

black girl love

letters

Why is Z either at the bottom or the last line of an eye chart? I mean you would think it would catch a break for once and be in the middle if not at the top. Life sucks even for the alphabet and I should know because mine sucks royally right now. My sitting here staring at the charts and how to pamphlets in the doctor's office isn't going to make it less suckier.

As you might have guessed from the ramblings above I'm not the typical chick. Matter of fact I pride myself on being atypical. I'll try anything once and I will do anything once, twice if it feels good. That's part of my problem. I feel as if I have to taste test life even when I know it's going to be sour. Sour lemons taste good at least that's what the candy makers would have you to believe. I also have this tendency to leap first, sticking my hand in the fire, not to see if it's really hot but how hot or even better , how hot it can get. You see where I'm going here?

Mike was my fire. He was my own personal flame and yes he was hot, scorching even. Which initially wasn't really a problem or issue, you know him being hot and all because I'm gay. Or rather I was gay or is it I'm half gay or bi? Me, bi. Wow, damn near boggles the mind.

Either way when I met him I was fully involved in being gay. I had a steady girlfriend. Not my first one by any stretch of the imagination. I have been gay since that day in 1st grade, when Michelle Brown, gave me a piece of candy and a smile while asking me to be her best friend. I accepted and we were best friends and I thought much more till 6th grade when I attempted to kiss her. Funny thing was Michelle really meant just best friends.

No love lost really. We are still good friends and every now and then when the third bottle of wine kicks in she tells the story of me attempting to kiss her to anyone who will listen, mainly me. She neglects to add that I generally do try again after she tells this oft repeated tale. Sometimes I succeed.

Third line T O Z

Sorry lost track of things there for a minute, back to the story. Like I said when I met Mike I was fully gay, living with my girlfriend of the past two years. I had rainbow stickers and decals decorating everything in sight including myself. Butterfly tattoo on my left breast, thank you very much. I attended all the local and not so local pride events. I was also out at work. In other words I was being me. Oh and my family is great by the way. My mom even has one of those PFLAG t-shirts. I love to see her in it declaring to the world her daughter is so GAY. Hmmm wonder what she's going to do with that t-shirt now.

Here I go again off track, I can't focus today for some now known reason. Anyway Mike, my personal flame, started working with me around mid-June. I didn't feel a need to come out to him because he had transferred in from another department. Plus I was positive the local gossip mill was in full steam producing all the tasty tidbits on me before he transferred over. The first day he commented on the sticker affixed to my PC. The one that says, "Tell your girlfriend to stop calling me." It was a gag gift from one of my coworkers so I felt it appropriate to display at work. Sometimes being the token has its benefits. I told him the story behind it, he laughed and we moved on to becoming great work friends.

Fifth line P E C F D

Well at least that's what I thought we were becoming. I mean we did, become friends that is. Somewhere along the way we became more. It all started simply enough. He brought me coffee one day. He even remembered that I drank a grande cinnamon dolce latte extra hot with an extra shot on Monday's. I tried four shots one day and couldn't sit still for the next 24hrs. It was rumored that I was being considered for random drug testing.

Anyway I thought that was sweet and returned the favor with his favorite cup of joe a few days later. Soon we were doing lunch a few times a week and that segued into after work drinks and finally dinner.

I honestly didn't think much of it. He was a guy and I was a gay girl right? Heck even the girlfriend didn't think much of our growing friendship. She met him briefly at one of those company functions that you drag your house/significant other to if you plan on moving out of a cubicle into a corner office near the bathrooms and not the elevator. That ding noise is way worse than the flush sounds, though the occasional snatches of muzak isn't that bad. Golden oldies are great to hum to while pretending to work.

She thought he was cute and asked if he had a girl-friend. Her sister was on the lookout for husband number three. I knew he wasn't seeing anyone but I told her that he was involved. That should have been my first clue that maybe just maybe something wasn't right. At the time I chalked it up to not wanting my personal life to mix with my work life. Yeah, that was my reasoning, sounds even lamer now. I gotta add I can't stand her sister but that's another story best saved for any day but this one. Oh boy is she going to enjoy this day when it's all said and done. SHIT!

Deep breaths, deep breaths...okay I'm back.

Seventh line F E L O P M D

So like I said we did drinks and dinner on the nights when the girlfriend was doing her thing with the elite lezbos crowd that I didn't particularly care for. You know the ones who think being a lesbian is an excuse for not shaving their legs and armpits.

Back to me and Mike. We clicked for some odd reason. Shared things you know. I told him the good, the bad and ugly about the current relationship and the past ones. He sympath-ized by telling me his relationship horror stories. The tire-slasher comes to mind, along with banana in a tail pipe girl. I couldn't share anything close to those extremes though the one that took all my panties and bra's when we broke up came in a close third.

Over the passing weeks we continued our talks about life, love and those things in between. I don't know if I revealed more because he was a guy or just because he was... he.

I do know the first kiss caught me by surprise. Typically we did a quick hug on parting, every now and then a tight squeeze. That time was different, the hug lasted longer, the squeeze was tighter. As I was pulling away he... we briefly touched lips.

I don't know who was more shocked. I'm guessing me because he's a guy after all and I'm... I'm gay. I should have seen this coming. Attractive guy and attractive girl mixed with liquor equals combustion. I was blindsided by the barely there kiss and my reactions to what was nothing or rather something that should have been nothing, something that shouldn't have happened. A first for me, remember I'm the lesbian from first grade.

Ninth line L E F O D P C T

We laughed it off while blaming the wine, good conversation and the sharing. I ran home and made love to my girlfriend. Trying to replace the taste of male with the taste of female. It worked, at least for a few weeks, till the second kiss. This one couldn't be laughed off or blamed on anything. We hadn't had dinner yet, no real conversation shared and no bottle opened. We didn't pull apart if anything we pulled closer. Fifteen minutes of close...maybe more who was counting? I'm thinking I was. I wonder if once you pull apart and come back together is that considered a different kiss or part of the original kiss? Now that's something to ponder.

Oh well, looking back on it I could have put a stop to things. I'm not simple or slow. After the first kiss, I should have backed off. I didn't. I kept on meeting him for dinner, even increased the number of times we met. Explained to the girlfriend that Mike was going thru a horrible breakup and I was his shoulder to cry on. A shoulder that stayed over till after midnight on occasion. A shoulder attached to a head attached to some lips that just kept coming back for more taste tests.

Oh yeah did I forget to mention I was going to his house for those dinners now? It was cute. We would cook together. Laughing and talking about our day, like a regular old couple. Something we weren't. He even introduced me to a few friends that happened to drop by. Well it was really a planned dinner party hosted by us. It was nice and they really liked me. Didn't bring up the gay issue once, them nor I.

You know I really can't blame him for things that happened. He wasn't the one with a live in girlfriend. He wasn't the one claiming to be gay while kissing me and doing other things every chance he got. Yeah I said it "other things" because of course the kissing lead us to "other" things. Remember I'm the atypical chick. The one that has to taste test everything.

I liked the taste.

I feel like my "life time gay membership" should be revoked for even thinking that, let alone doing that. I don't know how I've managed to conceal what's going on for so long. I really, Jesus help me, don't know how I'm going to explain the little bundle of joy that's going to arrive in seven months.

You guessed it the card carrying lesbian is pregnant. Pregnant by a man, the old fashioned way. Just found out, hence the staring at the wall in total shock for the last thirty minutes. The throwing up every morning for the last two weeks should have been a big clue. I, no we, thought I had a bug. Turns out it's the nine month kind.

Congratulations! That's what the doctor said. My utter and total stillness followed by the tears may have clued her into this might not have been expected. Not even going to go into the wanted aspect.

N O S W E U Z

Double damn. I mean just fucking wow. This is so one of those time machine moments. I just want to go back six months. Hell just give me two months and a flat tire or a tank on E.   Anything to...I guess abstinence is the best birth control method. shit...

 Oh well time to get up and go tell... tell them both.

Mondays suck.

Last line Q

black girl love

meetings

She needs me or so she says. Every time I try to leave she pulls out the you are the only one for me, I'm sorry things will change routine. I fall for it each and every time while thinking, hoping and praying that this time it will be different. It isn't, it never is.

So here we are once again with me feeling locked out of love and accepting table scraps from a woman who can't love. I've tried to teach her how to love… even simpler still, how to love me. She's too bent, bitter and twisted from past loves and life to be receptive. Don't get me wrong, she tries for a few days sometimes weeks to give me her before finally going back into the old routine of just taking and accepting. I try for a few days, weeks even to pretend that we are building something before accepting that things will never really change. I eventually stop pretending that our relationship will change for the better with just a little more giving from me, a little more acceptance from me. It never does.

Which is why I am here, what is leading me to this, this being meeting a stranger for conversation and laughs. I never pegged myself for a cheater. Online chatting has led to offline meeting. The first for me one of many for her or so she says. She's single and doesn't seem to mind that I'm not, slightly scratching my head on that one. Does that mean she's a good person with an open mind and is really only looking for friends or does that mean she's a potential cheater? Then again who am I to judge or question the sanity of another when it's obvious I'm not going down the pathway of righteousness.

It's 2:45pm on a Saturday afternoon and I have perpetrated a lie for the last week to explain my absence from our home and from our relationship today. She accepted all the details of the whys and wherefores with no questions asked. No surprises there.

I didn't need to lie, just felt the need to. Does that make sense? I wanted her to question me. I wanted her to wonder why I wasn't going to be at home on a Saturday, our day. I wanted her to add one plus one and get three, the reality of our situation. But no, she didn't even blink as I added layers to something simple. I'm meting an unnamed friend for coffee. She knows all my friends. We might go to the movies afterwards. She knows I don't like movies and that she had to bribe me to attend the last one we saw over three months ago. We might do dinner. Dinner without her on a Saturday hasn't happened in three years. Why now? She let all the opportunities pass with nothing more than a smile. I would say an acknowledgment but honestly I don't know if she heard me.

I made sure she saw me when I left. I had on a new outfit, not picked out by her, not purchased with her consent, implied or otherwise. It was chosen with my new friend in mind. She said her favorite color is brown, any shade of brown. So here I am dressed in multiple shades of browns with a few splashes of orange and red thrown in for good measure. I even tied my locs back with a multi colored sash that appears to invite you to release them or me. At least that was the impression I got when her hand absently went to pull the trailing edge covering my left shoulder. She stopped midway.

She gave me a hug and noted the new perfume. I don't wear perfume but my new friend likes a certain scent so I thought I would try it out. She didn't squeeze any tighter, hug any longer or ask me to stay. She went back to our home office and I went out the front door.

Text message 3:45pm, "Is she pretty?"

I didn't bother responding. I couldn't answer the question anyway. I never made it to the meeting, 3:05pm found me sitting in my car, engine idling in the parking lot of the local coffeehouse I was supposed to meet her in at 3:30pm. 3:15pm found me driving off, not towards home but away from there and her and changes that I thought I was ready for.

She knew and didn't stop me. That's the thought that keeps me driving now, continuing the drive from her, our home and changes that I have to be finally ready for now.

black girl love

she beats me

she beats me
beautifully

threatens me with lashes
even when I'm good
and that's often

why be bad
when the punishment
is still the same

so I
like all good girls
fFall to her feet
when she enters
hoping for small treats
of tongue on skin
resting
in hollows
carved out by me

failing that
i seek touches of the painful sort
nails embedded where skin connects
in the oddest of fashions
covering areas never seen by the sun

blessed

tears falling
because she loves them
from me
because she causes them
in me

she loves me I think

that's why she beats me
beautifully

black girl love

locs

Scratching my scalp is a signal that she ignores at first. It's been a busy Sunday after morning church services, lunch with my family and grocery shopping for our family. I was a little tired and I know she was more than a little tired. Being a mother and my wife was a full time job. I'm slightly spoiled and don't mind admitting it. I complain out loud that my scalp has been itching me all week and that the new growth is really starting to look bushy. I follow that up with tugs on my locs as if that will showcase the new growth even more.

She pauses in the middle of doing our oldest child's head and asks me in slow measured tones if I want her to twist my hair. I respond with a grin and a quick shake of my head in the affirmative. She responds with a shake of her head and a slight smile, "Go wash your hair and after I put the kids to bed I'll do you."

I run out of the family room into our bedroom and master bathroom before she changes her mind. I undress with anticipation of her fingers in my head. She has these long artistic hands with nails kept short and neat. I don't like fake nails, never got the point of them. She indulges me in that.

I think of those hands as the water runs down my body imagining them on me, following the water trail. She moves slowly but surely in everything she does, walking, talking and fucking me. I try to tone it down as I remember I'm in the shower for a reason.

I quickly start rubbing the jasmine scented shampoo that she swears makes my locs more manageable into my scalp and hair, I can't tell the difference but hey it makes her happy. Lather, rinse and repeat three times she says and I do before doing the same with the matching scented conditioner. I like it better when she washes my hair too, but beggars can't be choosers. I finish up by washing myself with another scented soap that she prefers. Wash, rinse and repeat three times. I've been taught well in the five years we've been together. After the final round I quickly jump out, dry off and lotion down. This time with shea butter, something I prefer. I finish everything off with a quick towel wrap around the head before throwing on a t-shirt and shorts. We're in for the night.

I grab the remote to the stereo before sitting on the bench at the foot of our bed waiting on her arrival. It's our ritual wash, sit and wait. She comes up after an hour or so. During the hour, the towel has slowly started to slip down and locs are escaping. Water dripping down the front of my face because I didn't even attempt to rub my hair dry. Bad habit that I need to break.

She walks in the room stopping halfway in and stares at me. Her face saying everything that her lips are opening to say but then she stops, shakes her head again and continues into the room. Damn is the only thing I can think of, I wanted more of a reaction. She must be more tired than I originally thought, I open my mouth to tell her not to worry and that I will twist it myself but before I can she says, "Get on the floor Micki," in a not so nice tone as she walks past me. I slid to the floor and warily follow her with my eyes as she goes to take a shower. I know it's not going to be quick so I jump back up and grab a few pillows from our sofa in the corner of the bedroom in order to be more comfortable during the long wait.

She comes out of the bathroom thirty minutes later naked, brown skin slightly shiny from the oil she just rubbed into it. I could smell it drifting in from the open doorway, slightly fruity, papaya and mango combination. She sits behind me on the bench, grabbing the towel with one hand and my hair with the other pulling my head back as the two separate. "Next time you don't even attempt to dry your hair I'm going to let you twist it yourself, got it?" I nod, slightly scared to say anything. "Good," she responds.

Silence invades the room as she starts at the back of my head, drying first before twisting, moving slowly but surely… twisting and tugging, locs falling to my back while she works, as she does me. Slight pain but then again that's what I like. I open my mouth to ask for more, pain that is. She stops me with a harder pull, twist and tug as if reading my mind, knowing what I like and giving it to me. I breathe in slowly but surely as she continues working around my head. I can smell her now. Body heat rising from the slight exertion it takes to do me as she promised earlier, fruit and her mingling in with the added scent of my jasmine scented locs.

"Get on your knees and face me, I need to do the front," she breaks the silence with a quick command. I respond just as quickly. I get rid of the pillows I was sitting on and bow my head in between her legs as she starts on the front. Face to face now with the center of her, the scent of her invades. So much so that I don't notice the tugging and twisting anymore, concentrating only on what's before me.

Milk chocolate tinted breasts hanging, dark semi-sweet chocolate nipples tight and pebbled from the AC blowing cool air into the room, or maybe from doing me as she promised. I look lower past the smooth skin of her stomach crisscrossed in the faint lines of motherhood and can see her lips parting slightly as her body moves, wetness seeping slowly. Pussy. I see hers, know each line, each inch, could recognize it in the dark. If ever blinded by touch alone I can tell it from all others. Lips slightly lighter brown than her breasts with pink flashes, smooth, silky even, glistening and extended, thick, seeking each other as her body reacts to me staring, breathing on her and them. Her clit peeks out seeking more than stares and warm air from me. Ass clenching, thigh muscles bunching as she edges closer to the edge of the bench, to me. I move closer.

My hands, which were resting by my side supporting me slightly in my kneeling position, moved up to the bench of either side of her. She tugged harder. I moved closer. I take a deep breath as my right hand moves toward those lips, fingers sliding in silently as they part slowly. She exhales above me. I felt it on my scalp, warm and wet, above and below. In and out, tug and twist. We work together. I fuck her.

She does me as promised.

She finishes the front and continues holding my hair back with both hands as I move in closer adding teeth and tongue to the invasion. She pulls and separates my newly twisted locs in unison with my tongue running along the edge of her lips, sliding playfully around her clit, occasionally sucking inward above fingers that haven't stopped pumping in and out, seeking depth, warmth and wet. My left hand reaching up to pull and tug on those nipples that I've suckled on many times before. I hear her breathing, feel her breasts as they sway with me, resting on newly twisted locs, warm and heavy. Scalp open as her fingers scrap and tug from the root to the tip. The harder she pulls the more I give.

She was upset earlier so I know I have to beg forgiveness the only way I know how to... between her legs. I say I'm sorry for not helping with the kids as much this week on the down stroke as my tongue seeks home. I'm sorry for not drying my hair on the upstroke. She pulls and tugs, softly saying my name as she accepts as she cums. Cums hard against my mouth pulling me in, holding me tight, locs spilling as she digs into my scalp with those long artistic fingers with the short nails. Squeezing me thru it, telling me she loves me and us. I hear it all as she cums.

I can't wait till her scalp starts itching.

black girl love

breakfast

I go in every morning to eat. I go in every morning to eat and feast. I go in every morning to eat and feast on her as she fills my senses. Sights, sounds and smells. Never taste, though I can imagine what she would taste like, slightly bitter possibly with undertones of richness.

I sit at my usual table and I order my usual meal. Two slices of bacon, two eggs lightly-scrambled, one piece of toast barely brown with grape jelly and one glass of water and one cup of coffee, heavy on the cream and sugar.

We barely speak past a morning grunt and limited eye contact. She's busy, I understand. I'm busy feasting so the limited verbal communication works for both of us. One-word questions, one word answers.

"Usual?"

"Yes."

I watch her between bites. Attention on her as she deals with people like me, regulars and others not so much. I watch as she deals with those that want more than she can offer at 6am: Conversation, jokes and her attention. I watch to see who she favors this morning, today versus yesterday, making note for tomorrow.

I watch her hips as she glides from table to table, filling and refilling; feeding a nation, her hips thick and plentiful. Every now and then she spares me a glance from watchful brown doe eyes. Sometimes I wonder if she's making sure I'm still there or if she's just surveying the landscape of which I happen to be part of, a rock in a quarry.

"Refill, please," stated lower than the buzzing sounds of cooking, talking and living of the diner. I half expect her not to respond. She nears me. I can tell because her scent overrides the coffee, the eggs, the grease and the humanity. Deep, dark sensuous even at what is now 6:30am. I want to taste it in between sips. Chicory. I want to ask what the

fragrance is but I don't. She's busy and I'm busy.

One-word questions, one word answers.

"More?"

"Yes."

She pours quickly and moves on to the next regular

and some not so much. I listen to her southern drawl as she

gives them more. As they feast on her and she fills them up

for the day. She gives out the occasional smile, sometimes

teeth, mostly just lips. Full, bursting with coco powder,

outlined in cinnamon lips. She tosses out the occasional

acceptance speech along the lines of, "Come back again,"

with a touch of near realness. As they feast on her.

She nears. Chicory traces floating, roasted, mellow, robust.

Her.

One-word questions, one word answers.

"Finished?"

"Yes."

"Check?"

"Yes."

I count out the exact amount and debate on the tip. How full am I? Did she fill me up? She nears again and as she walks by running one finger, casually, quickly almost subversively from the top of my right shoulder down the length of my right arm; filling me up with one last touch. I am full. 25%.

We barely speak. She's busy, I understand.

black girl love

showers

She said she wanted to try something different,

something taught by me, learned by her. I agreed. Simple

really, showering in the darkness, something different for her

and well practiced by me. She was attempting to learn me in

small ways. I teach me well.

To get the full effect I tell her, everything must be

done in the darkness. Undressing while whispering

commands, she complies. T-shirt, bra, skirt, and panties all

fall to the wayside in an unseen pile. Socks last as the

coldness of the tile floor seeps in and the reality of darkness

overwhelms an everyday habit now highlighted.

What's next is thrown out in a low barely

recognizable tone. Amazing that a little darkness turns

an otherwise lion into a little bitty kitty cat. I grab her hand to

lead her to what, the shower area, night vision adjusting.

Water on and warming up as she stands there tensely as her other senses adjust. Skin anticipating the wetness of the water and fingers itching to experience the wetness of her.

I open the door and pull her in after me, she comes slowly. Gasping slightly as the warm, almost hot water hits her skin. Our senses adjusting even more as I turn her so the spray hits me first, her second. I see her smiling, thru the gloom. Unasked questions, rising, that only actions will answer.

I tell her showering in the dark is a lesson in learning yourself but today I'm going to teach her me. I tell her how I like every inch of my skin to be wet before soap is applied and how I stand for a few moments letting my troubles, real and imagined, wash down the drain. All this with my eyes closed.

Adjusting the water as my body becomes use to the heat, needing more at times, requesting less at others.

Senses adjusting.

I show her how I wash me by holding her hand in mine as I put soap onto sponge and then sponge on me. Something fruity that hits me almost as hard as the water, just as important. I slowly move her hand in circles over my neck first... suds trailing before falling into the unseen as our moving hands covers my shoulders and then my breasts. She takes over slightly here. I let her.

Round circles that get wider before coming back to start again. She in control now directs the sponge downward, still traveling in circles that widen still before coming back to their origination point.

Across my thighs and down my legs, the flow of her, the sponge and the water. She even asks, tells me, to lift my legs so she can wash my feet. She turns me slowly access varying wash and rinse. I let her.

Circles and dashes and long broad strokes. Hair lifted so as to get me squeaky clean. Legs pushed apart to reach all the places in between. Bending to her will as she learns me, adapts to me.

Waterfalls of wetness, caused by her.

black girl love

ignoring

Sunday afternoons to me are supposed to be quiet and restful. I tend to spend most of them propped up on the couch reading a book and listening to the TV. She does what she does, mainly moving around and making noise, disturbing my peaceful Sunday.

I ignore her because that's what she likes. I understand her and she attempts to understand me. I ignored her when she walked in, looking around, testing the waters. I ignored her when she sat down silently on her knees in front of me. I continued to ignore her as she took the remote and muted what was essentially background noise to the book I was reading.

I ignored the hands, her hands when they slowly crept up my thighs. Outside at first, pushing my oversized T-shirt up slowly. I couldn't stop her, didn't attempt to stop her. The t-shirt was hers, I am hers. She had slept in it the night before and her smell lingered, it was still slightly molded into her shape. Plus, you have to understand, I was ignoring her.

I ignored her as she leaned, bracing herself on my thighs while her hands moved inward seeking softer, wetter destinations. The book I was reading was interesting. Interesting enough that I had to hold it closer to my face to focus and read the oh so important words inside. The words telling the tale of seven cities, of he said/she said, punctuation marks and page numbers.

Page 120.

I kept ignoring her even when her warm breath washed over my clit. I trembled slightly but only because of the temperature contrast, nothing more, nothing less. I ignored her as her tongue reached out and taste tested the air down there. I kept on ignoring her even when those hands, her hands pushed my thighs further apart, forcing muscles to strain as she sought more clarity.

Some have to visually see the pathways they are traveling.

Fingers moving in closer, joining that tongue in taste testing, the warmer air down there. Her tongue slide in and rested on a hill while lapping at the lake below.

My book was interesting. Page 120.

I ignored her and I ignored me. I ignored the sounds I made when her lips sucked my clit in and laid it to rest between them, her lips. In and out, release, tug, pull only to be released again. I ignored the sounds made as her fingers, the one on her right hand… one, two, three entered me slowly. Up tempo, mid tempo, rappers delight.

Don't get me wrong ignoring someone is hard work that's why I was moaning, muscles straining. Hard labor does that to me. I was wet, sweating, all the same, labor. My hips were moving to the beat because it's easier to read to music. The beat her fingers were producing, especially the middle one. The one that kept touching that spot, kept tapping that spot. Tap…tap...tap...rub. Tap, tap, tap...slow and easy. Sensitive, I am.

I ignored her left hand as it crawled under my T-shirt, her T-shirt, and lazily drew patterns on my stomach before encircling my left nipple. She pinched, she pulled, she squeezed. I ignored all with only a slight gasp, again it was the temperature difference.

I kept on ignoring her while she kept on doing her Sunday afternoon thing, moving, making noise… me.

I ignored her till I couldn't. Til I couldn't hold back the moans, til I couldn't hold back the wetness and finally my climax.

Page 120… interesting.

black girl love

sometimes

Sleepy sex…
That's what's on my mind.
Sex that's slow and softly sensual…
No rush, no pace just contentment…
Knowing the end will cum.

I love our noon day meals.

She likes to wake me from my nap with a kiss.

Sometimes it's a kiss on the lips, she chooses which ones.

Sometimes she suckles at my breast till the sensations caused

by wet and heat and her break my slumber. After kissing or

suckling me awake she greets me with a smile. Almost as if

welcoming me to the land of the living, the land of the

sexually aroused.

We move slowly, together rubbing gently our bodies

align with one another. No friction, not yet. Temperature

increasing as body parts meet and greet, no friction, not yet.

She's taller than me, not that it matters. I'm thicker than her, not that it matters.

I feel her breath on my face. I feel her looking at me. I stay eyes wide shut because this is a part of my dream, this is dreamy and not my reality, not yet.

We move as one as she rubs her cheek against mine. As I move my hands from the middle of her back to her ass. Almost in sync, in rhythm. Slow beat. I inhale her, she tastes me. Sometimes the cheek she just rubbed, comingling us. Sometimes the side of my neck followed by a nip. Sometimes my bottom lip, testing the fullness. Sometimes my top lip testing the strength. Sometimes gently, sometimes not so. I let her scent take me to where she was, where she is.

If it's heavy with a trace of heat I know sleepy sex will be slightly more interesting. Pain is pleasure even when sleepy. If her scent is light with a hint of cool, like a summer breeze, then we will flow as one till the journey ends like fatted calves full of each other, meal well eaten, slowly. I like both, want both.

Today it's light. Good. I'm happy. Getting happier as her weight settles on me. Feeling the slight crush of her breasts on mine while letting her scent override my sleepy senses.

She loves me, she loves me not. I play with her locs, I play with her ass. Tapping that chant in both spots as I pull, as I push with fingers always seeking more. Those same fingers running along the crack of her ass are causing a chain reaction, causing her cheeks to clench and her hips to lurch forward grinding slightly into me. Sometimes, sometimes it hurts when she thrusts into me, as we become one.
Sometimes I like it, sometimes I love it.
We finally have friction.

Body parts merging friction, heat rising friction, wetness dripping friction. All from one tiny action leading to a chain reaction.

I pulled her closer, closer than before. My nails, she loves this, digging in with the pressure, with the slight urgency of wanting closer, closer contact. I open my legs so that she might enter. Thighs sliding apart, then together, comingling juices, scent and skin.

One.

As her lower body moves into mine, she lifts her upper. Demanding that I suck, suckle. I obey. I also nibble and lick and taste her round fullness. I love the sounds she makes as my mouth fills with her. I love her body as it twists attempting to get closer, to reach me, to reach inside of me. Her locs swayed as my tongue played, faster, rolling around her shoulders before curtaining me, us as she looked on while I pleased her.

She smiled when she noticed I noticed. I scored her back slightly, punishment. After all she did wake me from a nap. She smiled broader and gave an intertwined moan and laugh in recognition of me, of us. I continued to feast on her breasts, while she stroked and tasted what she could reach. What I allowed her to reach.

Hands searching for a home, she found me.

And I find her, her secret entrance... moist leaning toward wet, warm leaning toward hot. Open leaning toward me and my fingers as I explore her ass... hole. One finger there, others attempting entrance as my other hand keeps her cheeks separated, as my mouth holds her breast in me.
Feasting.
Pushing in, sucking in. Her body twisting more, not wanting to pull away from either sensation. I hold her in, into me.

She rides two, three fingers now while holding her breast up to my mouth so I don't let loose as she moves faster. Like I would. Like I could.
I love our noon day meals.

When enough is enuff and its time to finish what she started, she lets me know. She ceases motion, while focusing on me, eye contact. Delicious. I slid out and let her slide out. She climbs my body slowly, while keeping eye contact. I know what she wants.

Head firmly positioned I offer her a seat.

I reach with both hands to cup her ass cheeks, to gage the position, to place her better on her personal chair… my face.

The scent of her hits me first, not the light scent that lingered around her breasts. Not the light scent that trailed her neck and wrapped around her locs and the curtain that she produced earlier with them. No this scent is her, not found in a bottle. Heavy, seeping almost. Sex of course followed by a musk, again not light but memorable, traceable.

Then the wetness, the almost humidity, as she moves in closer to my lips with her lips. My tongue reacts and reaches up to meet her, them. Just the tip connects to her tip, her clit. Chain reaction. Her body shakes, her clit jumps to attention, her hands grab my locs, ready for the ride. We start out slowly, pushing the pedal lightly, pushing my tongue along the ridge of her clit. Sliding from there to her lips, parting them slightly for a mini-dip.

I love our noon day meals.

I taste her glossy wetness. Thickness coating my lips, my tongue. Thicker as I venture further in between her lips. Thicker as she pulls tighter, on my locs, forcing me in closer. Thicker as she pushes the pedal, speeding up the pace of her ride. Brake then gas, then brake, then gas.

Her clit wants more attention. So I suck, so I suckle. I roll the tip of my tongue along the crest, while using my lips to hold her in me, pulling her further into my mouth... if possible. Pressure points. She grinds into my face. Grunting and moaning... panting from the exertion of her ride. Oxygen is not a necessity for either of us.

Her pussy wants more attention so I give it. I give her one finger, slight gasp. Two fingers, slight moan. Three fingers and she gives me full wetness, full heat and her.

She rides my tongue. She rides my fingers. Brake, gas... brake, gas. More gas, no braking now. Faster. Moans coming, my name being called, my locs being twisted, my head being pulled into her comingling...wetness pouring.

The ride came to an end, sputtered to an end. I held her as she trembled. I held her as she slid down off of her personal chair and down my body. Kissing me, sucking my lips, tasting herself. Smiling.

I love our noon day meals.

black girl love

lunch

Breaking bread and slicing butter are two of the things we do together every now and then. Lunch. Never dinner and hardly ever breakfast. Every two or three months we commune over food.

Catch up on life, loves and possible heart break. We gossip. We laugh. We eat.

Today is no different, outside of it being slightly warmer than the last lunch which was at the end of winter. She was embracing the sun in a white t-shirt and short skirt. I was in my usual. We hugged as we always do and choose sides of the table to sit. I sit with my back to the door so as not to be distracted by others. I have the attention span of a gnat. I wonder if she knows I sometimes don't listen. I wonder if she catches me staring.

"I'm hungry so hurry up and decide on what you want." She says bluntly.

"Please, you know I always get the same thing here so the only one holding you back is you!"

"You should be more adventuresome, try a different side item at least."

"Are you buying?"

"No."

"Then shut it up and order since you so hungry."

"I've missed you."

"I've missed you to bud." "What's been going on with you? I see your posts on Facebook but I'm sure that's only half the story." I said with a smile all over.

We spend the next forty five minutes sharing. She talks more than me. It's what we do and I expect it and encourage it. Intelligent women turn me on. Something about the way she's throwing her hands around while

157

emphasizing a point or it could be the way she is making eye contact, again to emphasize a point, adds to it. Intelligent women turn me on.

So I listen even more, say even less outside of the occasional word or two of encouragement so that she continues to talk and emphasize. Eventually she winds down. We sit in the silence of us.

Briefly.

She smiles and relaxes even more in her seat. I copy her pose while thinking, she's not wearing panties. She never wears panties and yet she sits across from me with her legs slightly parted. Is she daring me. Wait, we're friends. Just. She told me once across another table that she hasn't worn panties in years, never cared for them and thinks them unnatural. I smiled then, similar to my smile now while thoughts flitted in and out of my head, naked thoughts that you shouldn't think about a friend. Just.

"How is she?" she asks.

"She is fine," I counter around a half grin. I've been waiting on this.

"Better?"

"Much better," I answer.

"How so?"

You had to be at the last meal. When I shared that she wasn't the best in bed but I loved other aspects of her enough to deal with that slight lack. She laughed then and is smiling now.

"Well, I took the time to explain better what I wanted."

"Really…What is it you want?"

"I used your phrase 'pain is pleasure.'"

A hearty laugh from across the table and I know I have her undivided attention now.

"So, that made her all of a sudden better?"

"No, we talked some more and then we did some more."

"Ah now that I understand, the doing part makes everything better. Can I watch?"

Another silence as I try to figure out if she's playing or serious. Her face gives nothing away and her body position hasn't changed outside of her legs opening slightly more. But then again that could be her letting "her" breathe.

"Quit playing girl."

A pause as she smiles but doesn't answer my unasked question. So I plunge forward.

"You know she's not going to let you watch. She already thinks we are fucking when we do lunch. She's probably going to smell my breath when I get home."

"Why would she smell your breathe when she should be smelling mine."

We both laugh and another silence falls on the table,

comfortable.

"Tell me something" she asks. "Why do we always talk about sex?"

"You exude sex," I answer without thinking. Her eyes get big. I think I've finally stumped her. Good, though not for long as I see her mind wrapping around what I've said, whirling.

"Okay," is her answer after a moment of silence. "I can live with that."

So we speak on sex. How sex makes the world go round and round. She details her latest and I listen while thinking, she's wearing no panties. She tells me how she likes to have pain at the moment of release while I wonder if she opens up her legs a little bit more will I be able to slip in, just a little bit, one finger, two fingers then three. I swear I can smell her over the food or maybe I just want to. Slight musk surrounded by sunshine citrus. We are just "friends" flashes after every thought.

I share as well, that's the whole point. I tell her all that makes me wet, gradually, again. Some things new, some things old and some things borrowed. She stores it for a later use, or at least I do. I tell her how pressure here, makes me feel something there. She wants to see or rather do. I laugh and silence once again falls on the table. The silence hinting at an end.

This is what we do, lunch. Two friends, sharing over bread long gone cold and drinks turned to water from lack of attention. Full. I stand and gather my bag, while helping her with her multitude of items needed to lunch with me, purse, jacket and shades. We hug briefly while swearing that the next time there will be less time passed and that we should hang out more, outside of lunch every three or four months. She knows and I know the truth. Lunch is what we do. We gossip. We laugh. We eat. We are we till next we meet for lunch.

black girl love

ink

i'm a writer
and
she allows me to..
dip my fingers in her ink pot
so that I can scribble poetic nonsense
that only makes sense to her and i

things like roses are red
and
nipples are meant to be bitten
and shit like when she smiles the sun comes up
and when her ass is up
hopefully the shades are down

so i scribble
and i dip
ink spilling
cause I like to write…
fast

about us and how
we love
about us and how
we fuck

grown folk shit
about bending
scratching
biting
spanking
strapping

licking
Eating

grown folk shit
about her
full lips
heavy breasts
rounded tummy, hips
curved ass

so i scribble
and I dip
ink spilling
cause i like to write…
slow

about us and how
we love
about us and how
we fuck

late at night
when the dogs asleep
and the cable bill
ain't been paid
and its dark as fuck

We fuck

slowly
naked
wetness
seeping
sweat

dripping
friction
causing

reactions

so i scribble
and i dip
ink spilling
cause i like to write…
mid-tempo

about us and how
we love
about us and how
we fuck

on a rainy saturday
with the tv playing
a slow jam in the background
cable bill paid

we laugh
an giggle
talking while licking
nipples
and
belly button rings
and placing new tats
on our backs
carving initials
and i love yous
on semi flat stomachs
and curved buttocks
and ashy kneecaps

with the tips of extended
appendages

making fuck faces
to the sounds of
"for only 2 payments of 19.99 this can be yours"

i'm a writer
and
she allows me to…
dip my fingers in her ink pot
so that i can scribble poetic nonsense
that only makes sense to her and i

black girl love

distraction

Work or lack thereof has me idling, mind in slow motion seeking distraction, waiting for it to come. I hear her as she approaches and distraction fades, being replaced with instant wetness. Walk tall and carry a big stick comes to mind except she doesn't need to. Pathway's clear and doors open when she passes, the click of her heels demanding admittance with each step.

I obey because I have to, want to, need to do what she says. The part of me that chimes only for her comes to life as she nears. Eyes following along as she closes the door to my office. Clicking muted as she crosses the carpeted floor to my desk, to me. Muted though my ears reach for the sound as my eyes outline each step she takes waiting on her arrival, four inches.

No words being spoken as of yet, not sure if they will. She's done this before, I've obeyed her before. I wait for silent instruction yet to come. She reaches my desk, pauses for a few seconds as if considering options, before pushing me back so that she can sit in the center on the edge. She sits and stares, I acknowledge by looking down. She hasn't given me permission to stare back, yet. Slowly she raises her legs and places them on the armrests of my chair. No panties. I get wetter, joining the wetness glistening where my eyes were allowed to stray.

Am I wrong for sniffing the air? Inhaling deeply before imbibing, similar to a wine connoisseur acknowledging aged to perfection. I follow where she has lead me, told me to go, silently. No words being spoken as I sink in, licking and nibbling on my daily distraction. Muted sounds from her falling like backwash, filling my senses as wet and her and heat and me join. Tunneling effect as I drill my tongue into her pussy, as she rides me without leaving the desk and I, in my assumed position, bear the weight of those thighs and those legs surrounding me.

I bear the weight of being her daily distraction.

She cums for me, shaking, thighs clenching, legs falling inward slightly pressing in and reminding me to hold steady, movements precise. Heel marks setting into grooves carved yet again, deeper.

She smiles slightly, when pushing me back, yet again, still smiling while swinging her legs, standing and adjusting her skirt. No panties. No kiss, no hug, no words yet spoken.

She walks away, clicking muted as she crosses the carpeted floor as my eyes outline each step she takes away from me.

My daily distraction.

black girl love

situations

When I saw her I should have ran. Actually I did, just not in the wrong direction. She stalked me, cornered me in a crowded room. Being honest the room wasn't crowded enough that I couldn't run or even walk faster in the wrong direction. The room wasn't crowded enough that I couldn't scream for help if need be. Not that I would, scream for help that is. She doesn't allow me to.

I could have easily joined a random group of women in a club where my adding myself to a group would be appreciated and accepted with open arms, amongst other things. That might have prevented what happened. Like I said I should have ran and I did run, just not in the wrong direction.

Hi and hello were exchanged as I was backed up and forced into a smaller space of her choosing. No touching as of yet, just intimidation via eyes and presence. Crowding.

mental turning physical as her hand found contact with my skin and with me quickly. Rubbing slowly and softly down my right arm as she moved in closer still, breasts touching thru clothes made thinner by the heat exchanged. I braced myself, expecting more because I know her and she, yes she, knows me.

Open your legs was whispered, I think, I hope because that's what I did. Begging and pleading with quiet eyes to do what we both wanted, what I needed, in public. The same hand that was trailing down my arm moved lower, seeking home she found me wet, hot and silky. One, two, three fingers sliding in accompanied by a gasp and a muffled moan, mine and hers.

Conversation buzzed around us as those around us moved and created their own scenes. Music louder, covering up my moans, I hoped. Did anyone look at us as they passed? Could they tell?

Speculation added to the wetness with a sense of wrong being oh so right.

Head bowed as locs covered my face and hers while clothing help to conceal what we did. Appearances can be deceiving as we appeared to be whispering sweet nothings in each other's ear.

Conversation is what we had with no words spoken. In and out she glided not letting go of me, of us. Breathing deeply in my ear in rhythm with her strokes, I focused on her and me. My scent slowly seeping upward as the wetness poured downward. She moving in closer as my knees weakened, posture slumped as I got closer and she gave me what I begged for, pleaded for when our eyes met across the crowded room.

When I should have run and I did, in the right direction.

black girl love

dinner

4:30p.m. incoming text.

"Wear a skirt, no panties and those heels I like."

I didn't respond due to being slightly taken aback by the request, no demand. She generally follows my lead. Does what I say, bends to my will. I can see that time and distance has changed her. At least for tonight it seems. In town for a few days I asked her to meet me for dinner. Six months had passed since the last time we met for dinner. Six months since we did things my way, the way we always had.

7:30p.m. found me waiting for her in the lobby of my hotel. Anticipation had me wet. No panties to catch the drippings. I was hoping the lining of the skirt held up to the evening yet to come.

She pulled up, I got in.

"Hungry?" she asked. Not her usual greeting of smiles and statements declaring me to have never aged and any weight gained being a beautiful thing.

"Somewhat," I answered. Keeping it short as I attempted to figure out what was going on with her. We drove to our destination listening to some neo-soul artist wailing about love lost, love gained and the sex in between.

"No panties?"

"Yes, no panties."

"Good girl."

This was said with a half smile and a half glance my way. The first real look from her. The look was followed by her hand, moving slowly from the center console to my inner thigh pushing the hemline of my skirt up and up some more. No playing, no teasing, no words. She stroked with one finger, then two. Straight lines from mid thigh to center stage, each time fingers lingering longer and longer in my wetness. No pressing inward, just a firm resting, testing and acknowledging.

I opened wider in response to the non question being asked. She entered one, then two fingers. She entered once, then twice more and more. Each time lingering longer, pressure now, from me as I pushed down, reaching for more. She didn't oblige, held back and repeated again.

"Hungry?"

"Yes."

"Good we're here."

Slightly in a daze as we exited the car and entered the restaurant, I wanted to ask questions but felt I wouldn't get answers. At least not verbal ones. We were seated, side by side with me squirming, her relaxed and smiling.

I attempted to switch things around and touch her, make her as unfocused and unsure as I was. She didn't allow it. She didn't allow me to touch her. Verbal and nonverbal commands issued. My hands above the table during dinner. No touching her without permission, life in danger permission. Speak, talk and laugh I was told. We are at dinner, enjoy.

She on the other hand could touch. She could lean in and out of my space, my body. She did in multiple ways and multiple times. She removed something from my left cheek, my scent lingering on her fingers and now on my face. The same hand rubbing my arm occasionally, absently rubbing my scent and her scent into me, moisturizing my skin. Continuing the wetness, the dripping.

Thigh to thigh, slight pressure, much heat. Clothes rustling with my skirt joining the heels, I was told to wear, in wanting to come off. She admired the material and commented on the heels. All this while stroking again the skin of my inner thigh while never quite reaching the spot that I wanted her to touch again.

We ate, she fed me small bites of her. She blew cooled breath on the overly hot pasta dish before spooning it into my mouth. Small bites of her. She buttered my bread and stirred my tea. Small bites of her. Dessert was shared, same spoon, same bite. Small bites of her till I was well fed and full and wet and needing my other needs met.

We departed the restaurant holding hands. She let me.

She didn't ask my permission on after dinner plans as we rode to her home in silence. No music, no touching this time. I wanted to scream and beg for release now not later. Though I knew it was coming soon. I hoped it was coming, that I was cuming soon.

We went inside her home, me following and by passing the living portion of the home straight into the bedroom. A look was shared as we entered. I stripped. She watched. I wanted to go slow and give her a show but I couldn't. It was taking all of me to not beg for what I knew was coming fully dressed, outside of the no panties of course.

I finished and lied across the bed waiting. She let me, wait that is. While she did what I couldn't do, strip slowly, removing every piece with almost loving care. As if it was the most precious piece of material in the world. I wanted those hands on me, with loving care as if I was the most precious piece in the world. I wanted those hands removing the last six months of non attention from her to me.

She talked as she removed each piece. Nonsensical things you share with "friends," a continuation of conversation shared over dinner. Work was fine, and she was possibly in line for a promotion. The car was due for an oil change and she was thinking of painting the kitchen yellow. I think I responded in a positive, interested manner. I say 'think' because all I could focus on was the gradual glimpses and final reveals of her chocolate skin in pieces. The semisweet chocolate of her legs and arms, the slightly dark bittersweet chocolate of her thighs and upper chest and the almost milk chocolate of her breasts, stomach and ass.

After she was finished revealing, silence invaded again as she moved slowly towards the bed, towards me. I felt stalked like prey as she crawled towards me on all fours, no smile present and like a deer caught in headlights I didn't move. I accepted my fate. She pushed me flat while at the same time removing the pillows from up under my head. I stared up at her, waiting. She let me.

"Safe word?" she finally asked.

"Banana." I answered with anticipation.

"Good girl." First kiss was a slight touching of her lips to mine. Chocolate traces.

"Miss me?"

"Yes."

"Good girl."

She smiled slightly as she reached to the left of me and grabbed the silk material permanently attached to that side of the bed. I flinched slightly as she tied my left arm down. The material was cold. She grinned as she tied my right wrist down before moving south and doing the same to both of my ankles.

Spread eagle, flying with no wings.

This was the first time for me, in this position at least. I'm usually the one tying someone down. I was the one who affixed the ties to this bed.

"Ready?" another question asked.

"Yes."

"Good girl."

More kisses in between body parts meeting. Kisses starting at my brow and moving down with breasts touching as she leaned in and over. Lips moving to my breasts, tracing patterns and spelling words. Stomachs rubbing as she settled into place between my legs. Hands trailing my thighs, middle section and arms as kisses moved lower becoming wetter, turning into nips and bites. Teeth marks becoming tats, lighting on past pathways. Hands turning into instruments of pain and pleasure as she squeezed, pulled, tugged, bit, licked and scratched her way up and down my body... finding spots of skin sensitive to warm breath and others begging to be wetted up.

I asked once to be freed, only once. A bitten lip was her reply followed by a slap, harder than the ones before. Nipples twisted, turned, bitten and finally licked when it all became too much. Blowing of warm breath, a reminder that she was coming back. All this while I squirmed and pulled and tugged for freedom, for release and wept, begging for more. She gave me more.

She sampled me as if I was her first and last meal. Taking deep sips of my juices and bites of my flesh, hungry. Devouring all exposed parts, turning me to get to those not quite visible. Right flank scored with first her lips, then tongue, then teeth and finally her nails. Imprinted. Repeat on the left with nerve ending anticipation. Slight changes in pattern were enough to keep me aware and slightly non-compliant.

I asked for release again.

After feasting on my stomach till I was in agony she moved towards the center of me, my pussy, my clit. Slowly almost warily as if fearing me now. She laid her head on my mound. Smelling me first. Commenting out loud on the strength of my scent, how it clung to her fingers during dinner, how it enveloped her now. Sharing with me how she wanted to lick her fingers, then me, comparison shopping. She commented on my wetness, then and now.
Finally she was quiet. Resting.

I was slowly coming apart, every nerve ending anticipating that first stroke, anticipating the climax soon to follow. There was no way I would last long and I didn't really want to.

"Ready?"

"Yes."

"Good girl."

I could sense the smile and then my senses went haywire as her tongue, the one that had licked and taste tested every patch of skin on me, finally touched my clit. Once. An up and down simple stroke,a testing the waters type of stroke. A I have come home type of stroke. I jumped, she was prepared with an arm thrown across my thighs, shoulders pressing me down. As she lapped again and again, short, long, and in between. In between my lips, dining on my essence, slippery slopes and rocky hills.

Five minutes, completion came quickly, too quickly. I screamed my release as she continued her dining. I falsely assumed the fun, the games were over. As she continued I had no choice but to assume we were just starting. She wasn't done.

Ten more, fifteen, twenty minutes more of her licking and nibbling while adding fingers in places visited earlier for much longer. Adding fingers in places never visited before. She rode me while I rode wave after wave of satisfaction.

Climaxing becoming the norm instead of the exception as every inch of me became over stimulated and she still gave me more.

I accepted. All eight inches. Strapped. Stroke. Stroke. Stroke. Faster and slower, our bodies, our breaths. Thighs clenching, bodies blending as she whispered in my ear, into my pussy how this was us. Six months, six years of us. I accepted her declarations while making some of my own as I raised up, up thrust to meet her. We rode together. I saw light and stars as she rode me to her completion and my final moment of glory.

"Next time we'll have paddles and whips for dessert." I don't know who said it.

black girl love

dating

They wanted a date, a chance to explore other paths not

traveled. They wanted a date with me. I agreed. Clarise and

Michelle, a couple on the verge. Endless dreaming and

conversations found them placing an ad on

adultfriendfinder.com

2Hot2Handle
WE are seeking YOU for 3Play.
Be free. Be sincere. Be open. Be willing.

I liked the simpleness of the ad along with the

understated rules. My need for something different and as far

from vanilla as I could imagine helped me find them. Emails,

pictures and phone calls lead to a meeting of sorts. We

clicked.

We all agreed to lick.

A black-tie event was our first three way date and arriving together hand in hand was part of that. Eyes following, whispers trailing three women all attractive in their own way. Wouldn't you stare? Art on display with music flowing from the corner soft and subtle. Grown folk. Then I spot HER. The last one, the last one I loved and the last one to break my heart. She was also the last reason for me seeking something different.

We meet in the middle of a corner. Eyes locked before polite society rules surface. Thou shall not stare at daggers, sexual or otherwise, at a charity function. I wait. I win.

"So which one are you fucking?"

"The correct question is 'which one are you going to fuck?' and the answer to that is both." I answer with the purr of a well satisfied kitty. I loved her reaction. It was slight but powerful. Eyes widen, heat seeking missiles. Mouth tightens around the oh so fake grimace/smile she is showing the world. She moves in slightly closer, intimidating. She still knows what I like.

"Both huh. How is it that you are going to fuck them both?" Barely whispered but hot. "The internet is a wonderful thing," again the purr. "They were looking and I was more than willing to provide."

"So this is what you do now? Cruise the net for sex?"
I laugh caustically. "Please don't act like we never talked about doing the exact same thing.

Remember D?"
Slight relaxing in her posture was the only answer I got. No surprise there, admitting anything was never her style.

"So how long has this been going on? Are they your first?"

"Aren't you nosey."

We stand there in silence. Her waiting on me to answer, me waiting on her to realize I'm not. I let my eyes wander over her. It's been over a year since I've been given the chance to do more than steal glances. Sexy could always be used to describe her. 5'4 in, 5'7 in hills, 5'8 when she wanted to go there and long slightly muscular calves surprisingly covered in a fine dusting of hair. Like some southern girls she didn't believe in shaving her legs. I found it surprisingly sexy, the way the hairs would lift when I ran my hand up and down her legs before throwing them over my shoulders. She was dressed simple enough in a little black dress falling mid thigh, thick thighs. Honey suckle brown thighs, sweet. Ass, not quite apple bottom but not a pear with a slender waist, slides down smoother than a water park ride, like I said sexy. 36C's always erect, no bra needed, miraculous. Taste of chocolate mixed with a light vanilla swirl. Just noticed she switched to contacts versus glasses tonight. I preferred the glasses, intelligent women turn me.

Her hair is growing. Wonder who's washing it every Sunday

night now.

Without thinking or possibly thinking too much I

asked, "You wanna watch?" Not sure who was more

shocked, her at the question or me because I should have

thought of it earlier.

"Watch you and THEM?"

"Yes."

"Tonight?"

"Yes."

"Why?"

"Why not? It's something we both always wanted,

why not just go with the flow. You have to admit they are

attractive." We both turned to "them" at the same time.

Clarissa was a soft caramel sista on the short side but sweet

and thick with it. Thick legged, thick thighed and thick

fingered. I had plans for those fingers. Michelle was tall,

dark and handsome with loc's flowing past her shoulders.
Yes, handsome can apply to women too.

"Do you think they would agree?"

"Do you want to watch?"

"Yes."

"Then yes, they will agree." Going into an almost
professional mode I gave the details of our planned evening.
"We are going out to dinner after this, something light, before
heading to their home for the night. Call me after 10 and I'll
give you directions. If you are still interested." This said with
a slight challenge.

"Oh yeah, I'm interested and Toni," she waits while
I just look with a questioning lift of my eyebrow. "I'm going
to do more than just watch." Grown kitty walks away.

I go over to them and shared the change in plans with
a small smile followed by a group hug. Did you really think
they would say no?

We dine, conversation rushed, anticipation in the air. My phone buzzes, conversation and all pretensions cease.

"Hello"

"Directions please."

She arrives shortly after we do. I answer their door and take her to their bedroom. Power. Whose? We walk in. They are waiting, actually laying across their bed as tension fills the room. Wetness scents the room, theirs and ours.

I introduce them to her as pretend smiles fade, glances turn to stares and silence fills the room. The entire time a lil diddy plays in my head, *It's my party and I'll fuck who I want to, when I want to and how I want to.*
I start to speak as they and her jump slightly. Power.

"Let's get comfortable or in other words let's get naked."

They move off their bed, a king size four poster, centered in a room built around and for pleasure. Standing on opposite sides, Clarissa makes the first move. I knew she would. She kicks her heels to the side. I almost told her to put them back on but didn't want to stop the strip tease. Silk skirt slides almost effortlessly down her thighs and pools at her feet. She stands there for a second realizing all eyes are on her.

Power, hers for now.

I'm not sure I'm seeing her. Her body yes but her, not so much. The top comes off slower, soft skin revealed. Matching black thong and girly bra revealed. Stockings and garter, who would have ever guessed sweet innocent caramel dipped Clarissa dressed to impress. She came prepared to play. I glance at Michelle with a look that says it all, lucky woman, very lucky woman.

I stop her as she reaches to slide off her thong. "No, for now keep that on. Michelle it's your turn."

Ah ladies, a sexy stud stripping. Sometimes heaven can be found in your own back yard. She's uncomfortable. It's obvious. I'm sure she envisioned this evening being slightly different. When we met dominance was established.

I am.

She took off her black suit coat and laid it on the chair near the closet. Slowly she tugged her black dress shirt out of the waist band of her black slacks. Black on Black, that's a beautiful thang sometimes. Button, unbutton all the way down. It falls open revealing a nice surprise of 36C's encased in a black sports bra, six pack abs with enough flesh present to remind you of what you seek and who you are with. I wanted to lick each indention and remind myself later to do just that. She kicks off her black Stacey Adams and finally reaches for her belt buckle.

Ever heard the phrase it was so quiet you could hear a pin drop? Well I heard the scrape of metal against metal and every inch of that leather sliding out seeking freedom. Zipper, unzipped all the way down. She paused.

Power, hers for now.

Hands on her waistband, as she makes sure she has every ones undivided attention. The pants fall slowly down revealing black silk boxers. She removes her socks, bending over looking at us the entire time almost as if she's afraid to lose eye contact with anyone there.

Predators we were becoming.

"Stop." I say quietly as she reaches to remove her boxers. She does.

We all turn to her. She's been waiting but I think she thought the order would be slightly different at the end. No darling, it's my party I say with my eyes. "Next" is what I say out loud. She looks at me debating. I can see it and I can also see when she gives me what has been mine from the moment this evening was planned, last minute additions included. Power is mine. Control is mine.

She moves fluidly toward the right side of the bed, near Clarissa who tensed with anticipation. She smiled at her while placing her purse on the nightstand. I laughed inside.

That's my girl giving it to the end. She reaches up and behind, pulling her hair to the side as she releases the single clasp holding up my dreams. The dress falls.

They look. I've seen it many times but after a year my breath catches with them. For a second I wonder did she go home and change into my favorite on purpose but then I realize who I'm questioning.

No.

Black thong with a diamond encrusted L in the middle, black silk stockings encasing her long legs and thick thighs. Garter belt so low I'm wondering how she's made it thru the night. The thighs have it is the answer. That's all. She doesn't need more. She keeps the heels on, she knows me.

Again I smile.

All eyes turn to me and I give them all.

I smile and envision a soft light centered on me as I slowly remove my heels. No kicking them off for me. I like to bend and sway, a willow tree ain't got nothing on me. I put them to the side as I move back to the upright position. I see she is touching her slightly almost as if the wind is blowing thru the room and their bodies are leaves in the trees.

I have on a simple one piece as well, simple from the front at least. The back was out, missing… gone. I love that dress, the two sides of me in one. She picked it out a long ago. I to have to reach up to release their dreams, mine was in ribbon form. The top drops first revealing me. I am who I am. She stops touching her.

The waist is gathered so I bring my hands down and tug slightly, push gently and it falls. Again I am who I am. Naked now. Nothing. They were shocked but she wasn't, pleased definitely but not shocked. We enjoyed their shock, enhancing our pleasure. I enjoy being naked almost as much as I enjoy being the center of attention. She knows that. It's why I'm here, why she's here.

I move to Michelle. I have to take what some would assume to be the obviously dominate one out first so as to make sure the others fall in line. She straightens as I approach slightly wary but waiting, wanting. I can see it on her face. Eyes wide, mouth slightly open. Wanting me, to conquer me, but she can't. You would have thought she would have figured that out by now. Oh well, time to teach and learn.

I reach out in mid step touching lightly her face, right cheek. I can tell she's surprised. Could tell she wasn't expecting gentleness. She really needs to learn a lesson. I smile before I strike. Quick hard slap, surprisingly she buckled. Went to her knees as if a mighty warrior was struck down, in her prime, on the battlefield. Her reaction made me wetter.

Out of the corner of my eye I could see Clarissa jump as if to protect her mate. My ex mate stepped in to stay her. Not to aid my cause of course but now that she was pressed against her it was certainly easier to move her forward and onto the bed.

Michelle whimpered as I smiled again. She's such a pretty girl with long hair that twirled around the fingers of my left hand. Hair giving and tightening as I used it to pull her head closer to me, aiding me in keeping her on her knees. My right hand reaches out again. She flinches slightly, in anticipation, in fear. Who knows, not that it really matters. Slap again, harder and slower. Her body moves again this time absorbing the blow. A succession of quick slaps, some hard, some not so. Mouth opening and closing, slight sounds escaping. Dominant no longer, lesson quickly taught.

I pull her up by the same long pretty hair. On her feet, upright, she's taller than me but only in the inches recognized in the physical by man. Eyes remaining lowered as I tell her how pretty she is. Tensing as my hands flowed across her body, touching and teasing. I laughed outright before biting her right nipple. Pulling her closer, suckling in between licking, teasing tips, before switching sides, scratching sides, flanks, stomach and buttocks while pushing her onto the bed.

Joining she and Clarissa who were already on the bed. Yes, Clarissa and her had their own lessons going on. Clarissa was learning to be flexible, bent over ass up legs stretched far apart as she was spanked by her, hands only. Not too hard mind you, just enough to teach. Breaking her in slowly as you would any pet… a pretty picture as their heads almost touch as she and I do and teach. Me on Michelle and her on Clarissa, our eyes meeting across the bodies, we smile.

I continued teaching Michelle. Access granted to everything as she lied spread eagle on the bed, legs dangling over the edge, accepting anything and everything. I give her what she's always wanted, the chance to be accepted, to be dominated. Fucking her hard, pain and pleasure mixed. I tasted her entire body, enhanced her senses as I opened up pores long ago closed to this is what a masculine woman should do and allow only. I scraped skin, with teeth and tongue eliciting pleasure from areas never experienced. She came slowly, exhaling even slower with a release many times longed for. Next to Clarissa, who came hard and loud, exhaling in the middle of a scream. She's good at what she does.I looked at her and she looked at me. We smiled before kissing lightly above their heads, scents mingling. We still had it. Power.

thank you for helping make a black girls dream happen

CPSIA information can be obtained
at www.ICGtesting.com
Printed in the USA
LVOW03s0850110617
537715LV00009B/285/P